"Pastor Dan, you take good care of this little missy over at the parsonage,

while I work on her Harley," the mechanic said.

Pastor Dan? The *parsonage*? It couldn't be. It just couldn't. Smothering a groan, Faith raised her horrified gaze to find her handsome rescuer, Daniel Whitman, studying her. She'd swear she saw amusement in his sky-blue eyes.

"I think you'll find the parsonage to your liking," he said.

Faith leaned to retrieve her backpack, but her Good Samaritan had already reached for it. His hand closed over hers, and suddenly the air seemed electrified.

Her breath unsteady, Faith stepped back. If only Dan weren't a man of the cloth.

Then she squared her shoulders. No matter how attractive this small-town preacher was, he wasn't going to change her mind. Not about him *or* God. No, sir, it just wasn't going to happen....

CYNTHIA RUTLEDGE

wrote in her diary at age sixteen, "I don't know what I would do if I couldn't be a writer." Although this dream was shoved aside while Cynthia pursued a career in health care—first as a nurse in a variety of settings including hospice and, most recently, in the area of managed care as a Regional Consultant for an insurance company—it never died.

With the support of her husband and daughter, she decided several years ago to start writing and try to make her lifelong dream a reality. *Unforgettable Faith* is the result. Set in her home state of Nebraska, she says the story exemplifies the kindness, generosity and Christian caring of the state's residents.

Unforgettable Faith
Cynthia Rutledge

This book belongs to:
Angela Hare

Love Inspired®

Published by Steeple Hill Books™

STEEPLE HILL BOOKS

Steeple
Hill™

ISBN 0-373-87108-2

UNFORGETTABLE FAITH

Printed in U.S.A.

To every thing there is a season, and a time to every purpose under the heaven.
—*Ecclesiastes* 3:1

To my mother, Irene Ehrlich,
now with God but forever in my heart.

To my critique group:
Chery, Diane, Louise, Melissa and Sandy,
for all the help and advice.

And to Anita Evans for Aunt Dora.

Chapter One

It was a crime to have eyes that blue.

Even at this distance, Faith couldn't help but gawk. With hair the color of sun-ripened wheat and eyes bluer than any sky, the man embellished the earth tones surrounding him. And with every foot her Harley ate up, the increasingly sharper detail only confirmed her initial impression.

The cycle's savage roar reached his ears and he jerked upright. His penetrating gaze pierced the distance between them and a shiver of excitement rippled down her spine. Dimples flashed as if he sensed—and enjoyed—her reaction. One arm rose in the friendly greeting of one stranger to another in this part of the country, and he confidently stepped to the edge of the pavement. So close, she could have reached out and touched him.

Instead, she avoided his gaze and cruised on. His hand dropped to his side and the enticing smile faded. A wistful expression reflected back from her rearview mirror.

The disappointed little-boy look unexpectedly tugged at her heartstrings. An odd sensation welled in her chest and Faith wondered what would be wrong with taking a few minutes out of her not-so-busy day to stop and visit.

This was rural Nebraska—not Kansas City—and she'd already found the natives to be a friendly sort, even to a leather-clad stranger. Of course, it wasn't the kind of thing she'd usually do. But then her life hadn't been usual for a long time now.

Impulsively Faith inched the throttle down. Thanks to the flat stretch of roadway and her trusty mirror, she managed to keep him squarely in her sights. She cramped the front wheel to the right and started to turn when a swath of neon pink caught her eye. The brightly clad body moved at a snail's pace down the farm lane toward the mailbox. Headed straight toward her golden-haired Adonis.

Self-condemnation rose like hot road dust in her throat and she jerked the bike straight. Would she never learn? Of course he'd be married.

Resisting the urge to steal another quick glance, Faith forced her gaze to the road ahead. Only a fool would look back. And Faith Richards was nobody's fool. Not anymore.

Effortlessly the Harley sailed down the secluded

road. Dry leaves, yellow and brown, blown from a stand of old elms, crackled under the spinning tires. The keen fresh country scent of autumn in the heartland intermingled with the smell of approaching rain. Faith inhaled deeply, her senses wide open, thoughts of the handsome stranger vanquished by nature's beauty.

Reveling in the moment and the glory of the day, Faith pushed up the helmet's visor and let the sun's warmth kiss her bare face. A deer bounded through a newly harvested field adding just the right touch. She smiled and reached to straighten the chrome-edged mirror, taking her eyes off the road for just an instant. Just long enough for the creature to spring onto the highway, right in the Harley's path.

Her heart slammed into her throat. With a reflex born of fear, she clenched the handle-grips and wrenched the cycle to the right. Hard.

The buck bounded to safety. Faith lost control, the bike sliding sideways. Panic spurted through her veins. A left-over-from-winter pothole caught the front wheel and the Harley bucked Faith from her already-precarious seat, throwing her through the air to crash with a soft thud in the mud of a roadside drainage ditch.

Flat on her back, Faith struggled to pull air back into her aching lungs. For the briefest moment she thought of praying but pushed the thought aside and concentrated on getting her breath back. Agonizing minutes passed. She tentatively moved her arms.

Then her legs. Thankfully she appeared to be in one piece: bruised but not broken. Faith gritted her teeth and pushed up from the soil, an inadvertent groan escaping her lips. She ignored her aching limbs and crawled hand over fist up the steep embankment to the concrete highway.

She stared in shocked silence. The once-beautiful bike lay sprawled on the asphalt. A majestic vehicle transformed into a pile of rubble. One wheel cocked and slowly rotating in the air. Her heart sank with each step forward.

All because I couldn't keep my mind on the road, Faith thought with disgust. Her hand stilled the spinning tire, freezing against the hot rubber. A faint whine rent the air.

She listened intently for several seconds before she heaved a relieved sigh. It looked like she wasn't going to have to hoof it after all.

Praise the Lord.

Faith bit her lip, shocked she'd even considered voicing the once-familiar words. The knock on her head must have affected her more than she realized.

The distant whine rose to a crescendo. A rusty red pickup crested the hill. The reflection of the midday sun shone bright against its windshield, the glare blinding in its intensity.

Blinding—the driver?

Her legs, shaky from her tumble but still functional, now quivered and refused to budge. Like her worst nightmare come true, Faith could only help-lessly watch the truck hurtle straight toward her.

Her heart beat double time. Would she die quickly? Would there be pain? Was this how it had been for her parents?

A squeal of brakes split the air and the truck skidded, sending up a spray of leftover gravel. Faith scrunched her eyes shut and braced herself for certain impact. The buzzing in her head drowned out everything else.

Strong arms grabbed and held her upright. Thick fingers encircled her bruised limbs like a vise.

"What were you thinking?"

Her eyes snapped open.

"Don't you know better than to stand in the middle of a highway?"

She stared in shock.

"You could have been killed!"

Stared at the muscle flicking angrily in the square jaw.

"The sun was right in my eyes!"

Stared at those familiar eyes, now a steely gray.

"It was a miracle I even saw you. Lucky for you it clouded over for a minute." Taking a shaky breath, he took off his ball cap and used it to wipe his sweat-laden brow.

She tried to tell him she didn't believe in miracles. But what would he think if he knew *he* had caused her accident? Or rather, her daydreams of him.

In confusion, she turned her gaze away and focused on the dusty snakeskin boots, the worn Levi's and the faded blue T-shirt that made this apparition all too real.

"Miss—" His deep voice reverberated through her fog. The anger in his tone was abruptly replaced by concern. "You're bleeding."

She reached automatically for her aching brow, now wet and sticky. "Oh, my…"

"Here." He forced a wrinkled handkerchief into her hand. "I think you'd better sit down."

"I'm fine," she murmured, pressing the pristine white cloth to the knot on her head.

"I doubt it. You're white as a ghost."

She lowered the handkerchief. Her stomach churned at the sight. The once-white square was now soaked with dirt and blood. "Maybe I'm not so fine after all."

"C'mon, you'll feel better if you rest for a while." He placed one hand firmly under her elbow and propelled her across the pavement and into his truck.

He shoved aside some cleaning supplies with a sweep of his hand and gently released her to the comfort of the vinyl. She leaned her head back, quit fighting the dizziness and let her lids drift shut. They'd barely closed when warm breath on her cheek fanned them open.

"Thank God." He heaved a sigh of relief. "For a moment I thought you'd—"

"Died?" She blinked him into focus.

He nodded.

She thought about it for a moment. Blissful rest. No dizziness. No aches and pains. No problems. "The sight of blood always does a number on me."

"Then you'll be glad to know the bleeding has stopped." Two tiny lines of worry remained between his eyes. "I need to get your bike off the road. Do you think you'll be okay for a few minutes?"

The Harley. Pain worse than any physical ache seared her heart. She waved aside his questioning look. "Sure. Go."

By the time he returned and slid behind the wheel, raindrops splattered the dusty windshield and the sun had once again played its disappearing act behind the clouds.

She glanced at the darkening sky. Visions of a monsoon sweeping the bike away swam in her head. "My cycle—"

"I took care of it."

"But—"

"Have a little faith," he teased, as if trying to lighten the air. "No need to be a doubting Thomas."

How did he know?

"It's off the road. Once we get into town, I'll send someone for it." He shot her a quick grin and eased the vehicle into first gear. "Trust me."

"I don't even know you."

"Sorry 'bout that." His fingers tipped the brim of his cap. "I'm Daniel Whitman, but most people call me Dan. And you are—?"

"Faith Richards."

Something flickered far back in his eyes. "Nice name."

"Thank you."

"It's also a beautiful thing," he added.

"What is?"

His smile broadened. "Faith."

She groaned to herself. *Faith indeed!*

"I think I'll just rest my eyes for a bit."

He shook his head. "Not a good idea. I don't know much about first aid, but I do know you need to stay awake. At least for now. We'll talk on the way. It'll keep you awake."

He cocked his head and gave her a quick glance. "You're not from around here, are you?"

Faith shot him a glance out of the corner of her eye. "How'd you guess?"

Dan lifted one shoulder and the corner of his mouth quirked upward. "Just a hunch."

He turned his attention back to the road and she studied him, finding the firm features and the confident set of his shoulders very much to her liking.

"Do you and your wife like living in the country?" she blurted out, a warmth creeping up her neck at her uncharacteristic boldness.

His lips twitched. "What makes you think I'm married?"

She twisted her finger around the handle of her bag and kept her gaze focused downward. "Well, surely you don't live all alone in that big house back there."

Realization lit his features. "Oh, you thought I lived at…" He shook his head. "I was just picking up the mail for a friend."

"The friend in the pink shirt?"

Dan's gaze stayed focused ahead but he chuckled. "Harold decided when he turned eighty that bright colors were the spice of life."

Harold. Faith breathed a sigh of relief, wondering at the same time why she even cared if this friend was a woman or a man. "So, I take it you and your wife live in town?"

A dimple flashed briefly in his cheek. "I don't have a wife. No time for one. How 'bout you?"

"No, no wife for me, either." Faith attempted a chuckle but it came out as a heavy sigh. No husband. No pets. No one. "Mr. Whitman, I'm sorry I've caused you so much trouble."

"Call me Dan," he said immediately. "And, as I said, it's not a problem." He eased off the accelerator and he slowed to turn. "Cleaning can always wait."

"What were you cleaning?"

"The church. We usually do a major overhaul at least twice a year. Usually in the spring and fall."

Faith stiffened and a cold shiver ran down her spine.

"The youth group is scouring both the church and the parsonage from top to bottom. The kids are doing their Christian duty today—" he glanced sideways as if to see her reaction "—and I'm doing mine."

"Being the Good Samaritan," Faith muttered.

He smiled with approval. "That's right."

Oh, great, thought Faith, just what I need. Somehow she'd never thought to connect Dan Whitman and religion, despite that crack about being a doubting Thomas. It simply hadn't crossed her mind.

"Maybe you'll get a chance to worship with us on Sunday," he said, deepening her disappointment. "It's a great congregation."

Faith kept her face impassive and listened to this Adonis rattle on about the church all the way into town. She let him talk. Why not? The man really meant nothing to her despite the way his rugged good looks had stopped her in her tracks and made her heart pound. Besides, she'd be long gone by Sunday. And even if repairs to her Harley took longer than she thought, it wouldn't matter. She'd already made up her mind before leaving home.

Faith Richards wasn't going to set foot in any church ever again.

Chapter Two

"C'mon, Faith, tell the guys here how you happened to wreck this fine machine." Ray grunted around the short, fat stogie in his mouth. The mechanic's grease-stained hands ran affectionately over the Harley.

Faith bit back a smile and gazed around the group of eager faces surrounding her.

Apparently word spread quickly in a small town. And a female biker was big news. Just since she'd arrived at Ray's Garage, five men had dropped by. They stood, shuffling their feet, throwing her surreptitious but fascinated looks from the corners of their eyes.

"Tell them about the bit of trouble you had." Again the mechanic caressed the bike with a loving touch.

The men's eyes widened. They seemed friendly enough, concerned and eager to get a firsthand report of the accident. The one thing Faith's background as a drama teacher had instilled in her was the need to rise to the occasion. Especially when you had an appreciative audience.

"Bit of trouble!" Faith's eyebrows shot up in mock surprise, astonishment in her voice. "You call slamming into the pavement and ruining a brand-new Harley-Davidson motorcycle a bit of trouble?"

Faith leaned forward in the intimate manner of a master storyteller. If they wanted a story, she'd give them a whopper.

Moments later her voice rose dramatically at the tale's climax. "Suddenly it leaps out! I react immediately with all the skills at my disposal, but it was too late. And the Harley and I—" she paused dramatically and heaved a theatrical sigh "—go down together."

"Just like the *Titanic*." The sound of rich laughter rang in her ears.

Faith glanced in the direction of the familiar baritone.

"She's right, Ray. This lady has certainly had more than just a bit of trouble."

Her eyes were nearly blinded by the light behind the man in the doorway, but she'd have recognized those broad shoulders anywhere. He'd returned, just as he said he would. Her heart skittered in her chest and her lips curved in a welcoming smile.

"Looks like your ride is here." Ray nodded a welcome to Dan. "And our break is over. We best be gettin' back to work. I'll just give you a call over at the parsonage when it's done."

Faith frowned. Ray had mentioned something about that earlier, but she'd just dismissed his comments. "I told you, I'll be staying at a motel while I'm in town."

"Missy, I think those pain pills have done gone to your head." The mechanic shook his head, the cigar still tightly clenched between his teeth. "I told you earlier, there are no motels in Willow Hill. The parsonage is it."

Faith's head started to throb. She was doing her best to get away from God, but He apparently had something else in mind. "I don't want to put anybody out."

"The little lady can stay with me. I'll make some room in my trailer." Hank, the man with the bushy mustache, leered suggestively. The doughnuts she'd just devoured formed a hard lump in her stomach

"Now you just hold on a minute, Hank," Ray sputtered. "She'll be stayin' with Aunt Dora. There's nothing that gives that old woman pleasure like feeding and fussin' over someone."

Faith looked up in surprise. "You didn't tell me your aunt lived at the parsonage."

The little man stared, astonishment blanketing his face. "Why, I guess I just assumed Dan told you."

The sight of Hank licking his lips made her decision easy. "Okay, I give up. I certainly wouldn't want to disappoint your aunt."

"Good. The parsonage it is. Pastor Dan, you take good care of this little missy. I like her. And you—" for the first time Ray actually took the cigar out of his mouth "—you don't worry your pretty little head about that big Hog over there. Ol' Ray'll take good care of that bad boy. You can count on it."

The parsonage. Pastor Dan. It couldn't be. It just couldn't be. Smothering a groan, Faith raised her horrified gaze to find Dan studying her intently. And if she didn't know it was impossible, she would have sworn she caught a hint of amusement lurking in the sky-blue depths of his eyes.

"I'm glad you changed your mind, Miss Richards. I think you'll find our parsonage very much to your liking. And, as Ray said, Aunt Dora will be thrilled."

He held the outside door open for her. For a moment she hesitated, tempted to ignore him. But she'd spent her whole life respecting ministers and, as much as she'd like to, she couldn't stop now.

Faith leaned over to pick up her backpack but he'd already reached for it. His warm hand closed around hers and the stale smoky air suddenly seemed electrified. Her gaze jerked to his. Emotions reflecting her own played across his face.

Her breath unsteady, Faith pulled away and stepped back. If only he wasn't a man of the cloth....

Faith squared her shoulders. No matter how attractive or dedicated this small-town minister was, he wasn't going to change *her* mind. Not about him or his God. No, sir, it just wasn't going to happen. Not if she had anything to say about it.

By anybody's definition, the parsonage—his home—was a mansion.

Built by the founder of Willow Hill, no less, over one hundred years before, the imposing Victorian loomed over all the other structures in the small community. From its wraparound porch with swing, up to its turret gleaming with freshly polished windows, the place was all anybody could have wanted and more.

Dan ushered Faith to the guest room at the top of the stairs. A bright sunny room, it looked like it had been decorated with a woman in mind. Setting her bag on the bed, he waited silently for her reaction.

After a perfunctory "It's lovely," she moved to the open window and looked out. She paid no attention to him or the room; her entire attention focused on the street below.

Dan hesitated a moment, watching her in profile,

realizing he never knew someone who rode a Harley could be so beautiful. But then he'd never met anyone like Faith Richards before. From her disheveled ebony curls to her high exotic cheekbones to her milky complexion. Even those cat-green eyes. He tried to ignore all of these things and reminded himself that such an attraction would be perilous.

Dan cleared his throat and she turned around. "The bathroom is next door to your right. You'll find towels and washcloths under the sink."

"Thank you," she said, her gaze again drifting to the window. The girl who had entertained Ray's Garage with dramatic tales and laughter had certainly clammed up.

"Aunt Dora should be back any minute. She serves dinner promptly at six-thirty." He paused. "If you'd prefer a tray sent up, or if there's anything else I can do for you—"

Her gaze dropped to the Bible on the nightstand next to the bed. "Well, for starters, you can take that with you."

"I've already got one," he said. "This is for guests."

She picked up the book and turned it over in her hands. Her fingers caressed the surface of its black leather binding as if her touch searched for something unseen. She contemplated it for a long moment. Finally she handed him the Bible. "No, please. Take this. I don't need it."

The pain in her face belied the hard-boiled words. Beneath the façade she was trying so hard to keep up, Dan sensed her vulnerability. After all, that was his job. Beyond a doubt, this woman desperately needed God's word and grace in her life.

Something of his thoughts must have reflected in his eyes. Faith's jaw jutted out and her eyes flashed green fire. "Look, I don't mean to be rude. I really don't. But if being a Christian is a requirement for staying here, tell me now."

He shook his head slowly and replaced the Bible on the nightstand. "It's not."

She ran a trembling hand through her dark hair. "Da—Pastor Whitman."

"Dan is okay."

"Dan, I'm sorry if I appear short-tempered, but I really am very tired. You know—" she shrugged "—the accident and all."

"Of course. Well, like I said, if you need anything, I'm here for you, Faith." His gaze met hers. "Anytime."

He stepped out of the room and softly closed the door behind him. He started down the stairs, sorely tempted to go back and try to talk to her. But she was prickly as a roll of barbed wire. And as tightly wound.

Shaking his head, he shot a quick prayer heavenward and wondered just what the good Lord had in store for him now.

* * *

Still groggy from her nap, Faith swung her bare feet over the side of the bed. Delicious aromas wafted up from downstairs and she knew it would be only a matter of time before they called her to the supper table. Unfortunately, avoiding the man meant she also had to miss a home-cooked meal. Her stomach growled against its own emptiness, urging her to reconsider.

Dan seemed nice enough and he'd been the perfect gentleman, but his nearness made her feel almost shy, and that was an entirely new one for her. Coy and bashful she'd never been.

But Dan Whitman's look said he knew her. As if he could look right into her very soul. As if he liked what he saw there...

Nah. Faith quickly put that thought aside. The reverend didn't know her. Not at all. And she wouldn't be around Willow Hill long enough for him to get to know her, much less *look into her soul.*

With a renewed vow to keep her distance, Faith quickly showered and pulled on a clean pair of jeans and a shirt. She stole quietly down the front stairs and tiptoed across the parquet foyer, heading toward the front door and the safety of the outside. The old wood floor squeaked as if a herd of elephants were trooping across it.

"Like some supper, Miss Richards?" A masculine voice sounded behind her and she whirled. Even with his hands dusted with flour and his long legs clad in a ragged pair of jeans, Dan Whitman looked as handsome as ever. Maybe even better. "Aunt Dora's almost finished with dinner. She really outdid herself this evening."

"I don't know—"

He nodded his blond head toward the kitchen. "Oh, come on, you must be hungry. I promise I won't bite." He quirked a mischievous grin. "At least, nothing but the beef Wellington."

Faith smiled in weak surrender. Dan led her into the kitchen and she took a seat at the large wooden table under the window. Potatoes bubbled noisily in the huge iron pot on the stovetop. The smell of roasted beef crept out from the oven below. Dan went back to kneading dough for the biscuits.

"I'm beginning to think Aunt Dora is just a figment of your imagination," Faith said.

Dan plopped bits of dough onto a baking sheet. "She just ran next door to get coffee. We were out and she thought it would be nice if we had some to go with the pie."

"Pie?" Faith's mouth watered.

"Homemade apple." In a well-practiced move, Dan put the biscuits in the oven, shut the door and turned on the timer. "I picked the apples myself."

"You're quite the man. Baker, apple-picker—"

"Don't forget minister."

How could she ever forget that? "You don't seem like one to me."

"He's a wonderful preacher."

Faith glanced up at the feminine voice.

Tall and wispy thin, the woman stood ramrod straight in the doorway, a gnarled oak cane in one hand, a can of coffee in the other. Her snow-white hair and lined face complementing the wisdom reflected in the pale blue depths of her eyes.

Dora sat down as soon as the introductions were completed. She leaned forward, propped her elbows on the table and cast Faith an inquisitive glance. "We have a few minutes before dinner's ready. Why don't you tell me a little bit about yourself."

Faith twisted the napkin in her lap. "There's not much to tell."

"Are you married?"

Dan choked on his laughter. Faith smiled remembering her own not-too-subtle interrogation in the truck.

"No. I'm not."

"Ever been married?"

Faith shook her head.

Dora nodded her head, a satisfied smile curving her lips upward. "Where are you from?"

"Kansas City."

"My sister lived there back in the fifties. She was a member of First Bible in Overland Park. What church do you attend?"

Faith opened her mouth then snapped it shut. "I don't."

A shadow of dismay crossed the wrinkle-lined face. "Oh?"

Sweat trickled down Faith's back. Dora clearly expected her to elaborate. An uneasy silence descended. The clock ticked on while each waited for the other to cave in.

The timer on the oven rang and Faith heaved a sigh of relief.

"Looks like further questions will have to wait," Dan said. His eyes danced with amusement.

Aunt Dora stood and reluctantly picked up the oven mitt. "Yes, maybe we can sit on the porch later on. It's so good to have you here. I was just saying that it had been much too long since we'd had guests. God heard me and now here you are."

"God had nothing to do with it," Faith said smoothly and proceeded to give the woman a rundown of her accident.

"I'd say it's a miracle you came through relatively unscathed. It's just too bad about your motorcycle." The older woman clucked in sympathy. "You're welcome to stay as long as you like."

"Thanks." Faith bent her head and studied her hands. "But I'll be leaving as soon as my bike is fixed."

Aunt Dora looked up over the open oven door, her face flushed from the heat. "I'm sure those parts won't be in before Sunday. That'll give you a chance to hear one of Pastor Dan's sermons."

Faith squirmed. How could she tell this kind woman that she had no intention of sitting in a church pew this Sunday, or any other Sunday for that matter?

The phone saved her from the need to reply. Dan took the call in the hall, but even from a distance, she could tell something was very definitely wrong.

Grim-faced, Dan carefully set the receiver down. "That was the hospital. Little Joey Spanel isn't doing well." He reached over and picked up a well-worn Bible from the counter. "Don't wait up. I'm not sure how long I'll be."

"Don't you worry about us. We'll be fine. You just take care of Joey and his family." Aunt Dora waved him off with one hand, apparently not the least bit upset he wouldn't be there to enjoy the feast she'd prepared.

Saved from Dan's unsettling presence, Faith savored every delicious morsel and discovered a hidden benefit to hearty eating: with her mouth filled with food, she couldn't answer questions.

Instead, Faith listened politely. She learned the parsonage had been completely renovated in anticipation of Pastor Dan's arrival three years ago. Dora proudly proclaimed the kitchen was "top-notch" and fit for a queen.

"All this house, and Dan, needs now is a wife." Dora plopped a dollop of whipped cream on top of the warm pie and handed it to Faith with a sideways glance. "Dan's very nice, isn't he?"

"He seems to be," Faith said, wishing she could avoid this subject. "I'm sure he won't have any trouble finding the right woman. There's probably lots of women who'd love to be a minister's wife.''

"You're right about that. It seems like every eligible female in Willow Hill would like to wed our Pastor Dan. He's very handsome. The girls call him a hunk.''

Faith choked on a bite of apple.

"I do believe they're right," Dora said thoughtfully. "He's definitely a hunk. What do you think?''

Faith shoveled another forkful of flaky crust and apples into her mouth. "Umm-umm.''

"Hardworking, too. During the past three years, he's showered this congregation with all his time and attention. Thinks there's no time in his life for romance.'' Dora's voice clearly implied what she thought of that foolish notion.

"Have you ever considered he might be right?''

"Hogwash. He needs someone at his side. Sharing his life. My Herbert and I were married sixty-five years before he died.'' The older woman reached for another cup of tea, her bony hands trembling with age and emotion.

Faith glanced longingly at the door and wondered if this would be the time to mention a throbbing headache.

"Faith." Aunt Dora's pale blue eyes focused squarely on her. For a second, Faith wondered if the woman could read minds as well as she cooked. "I was wondering if you'd accompany me to church this Sunday. I'm being recognized for sixty years of service.''

The clock on the wall ticked away the seconds, the sound deafening. Faith frantically searched for a way to say no. Even though Dora had been nosy, she couldn't help but like the woman. She just didn't realize what she was asking.

"Sixty years. Congratulations." Faith forced a brittle smile. "That's wonderful. I wish I could be there, but I'm afraid I'll be on the road by then." Her gaze darted to the clock. "In fact, I should probably be getting to bed. Ray said there's a chance my cycle parts could come in tomorrow."

Dora slowly lowered her teacup. "Ray?"

Faith nodded. "The mechanic? Your nephew?"

A little laugh trilled. "Oh, yes. Wonderful boy."

"So, if you'll excuse me…"

"Of course, my dear, of course. Come and give me a hug. All of a sudden I'm quite tired myself."

The paper-thin arms wrapped themselves gently around her. For a moment Faith was sorry she wouldn't be able to go to the service. "It was a pleasure to meet you. It's too bad I'll be leaving so soon."

Dora's eyes twinkled as she held Faith at arm's length. "Oh, my dear. You never know. God works in mysterious ways."

Chapter Three

The afternoon sun shone high in the sky. Faith dressed quickly. She slipped down the back stairs and followed the scent of cinnamon rolls to the kitchen.

A piece of paper propped in the middle of the table captured her gaze. She grabbed a roll with one hand, reached for the note with the other and quickly scanned the first few words. She crumpled the paper into a tiny ball.

Ice Cream Social, indeed. She could think of a lot better places she'd rather be on a beautiful fall day.

She downed the pastry, licked the icing from her fingers and stepped out the door into the sunshine, ready for some serious exploring.

Willow Hill was a pretty, all-American town, almost out of a storybook. All white, clapboard houses, handkerchief lawns carpeted with green and picket-fenced gardens overflowing with hollyhocks, roses and daisies.

As if adding to the Norman Rockwell picture, up ahead two young girls strolled, their legs spindly above white socks and sneakers. Dressed in denim shorts and plaid shirts in autumn hues, their hair brushed their shoulders in soft curls. One a blonde, the other a brunette. They talked in high, excited tones.

They must have heard Faith coming up behind them, because they turned and stared at her, their eyes growing wide. Despite their mascara and pastel lip gloss, they looked about the age of the high school freshmen or sophomores Faith had once taught.

She'd planned to go around them, but they stepped aside and waited for her to catch up.

"Hi!" they chimed in unison, their smiles radiating innocence and trust.

Faith grinned back. "Hello."

"I don't think we've seen you before. Are you new in town?" The taller of the two girls, her hair a luminous buttercup-yellow, spoke for both of them. Pretty now, she would be beautiful in a few years.

"I'm just passing through." Faith leaned down to retie a lace that had come undone. "How 'bout you girls?"

They looked at each other and giggled. The sound rippled in the warm, fall air.

Again the blonde spoke for both. "We've lived here our whole lives. Where're you from?"

"Kansas City."

"I'd like to live there. At least there'd be stuff to do all the time."

"Looks to me like there's something to do here. You girls look like you're going somewhere important."

They nodded. "It's Harvest Days in the town square."

"Sounds like fun."

"My name's Tami. And this is Amy. What's your name?"

"Faith Richards."

"Well, why don't you come, too?"

Faith hesitated, glancing at their young, eager faces.

The brunette glanced at her friend. Speaking on her own for the first time, she whispered, "Tami's boyfriend will be there," as if that were some kind of inducement.

Faith raised her brows. "Oh?"

"I wish!" blurted Tami, then she sighed. "We don't know if he even likes me."

"Tami, last Sunday he looked right at you and smiled—"

Tami just shook her head.

"Is he cute?" Faith asked.

"Real cute." They both answered together. "You've gotta see 'im."

Faith couldn't help but smile. "Okay," she said. "Lead on."

Falling into step beside them, she listened to their chatter and wished she could remember when her heart was so young and carefree.

In only minutes they approached the town square. A banner at one of the booths gave Faith her first clue she was somewhere she didn't want to be. Willow Hill Community Church Ice Cream Social it proclaimed in black letters, big and bold on a fluttering span of white cloth.

"A church social?" Faith's heart sank. She could never get away from church doings.

Amy nodded. "It's part of the celebration."

Tami grabbed her hand and pulled her forward. "There's somebody here I want you to meet."

It couldn't be.

It was.

When the pastor turned in the direction of Tami's voice, Faith saw his eyes narrow at the sight of her. Then his face lit up in welcome.

Faith forced a smile as she strolled over. Today he looked different from the man she'd first laid eyes on. He'd shaved, slicked back his unruly curls and had abandoned the jeans for a pair of brown slacks, topped with a cream-colored dress shirt. He'd dressed the part of the conservative minister;

yet, as he adjusted his tie, the oh-so-respectable shirt couldn't hide the ripple of muscles beneath.

"Faith! I'm so glad you came."

"You know him?" Tami's gaze flew from Faith to Pastor Dan and back again.

"Faith is staying at the parsonage while her motorcycle is being fixed," Pastor Dan explained.

"Staying at the parsonage? With you?"

Dan laughed, a rich full-throated, husky sound. "Looks like it."

"Just until my Harley is fixed," Faith volunteered.

"Oh," said Tami, her eyes clouding with an inscrutable look. "I see somebody over by the gazebo. I gotta go." She pulled her friend away. "Come on, Amy."

Faith frowned. Something was definitely troubling Tami. Hopefully the boy she liked wasn't here with another girl. That kind of thing could be devastating.

"I wonder what that was all about?" she said.

Pastor Dan shrugged. "You know kids. Probably forgot she was meeting someone."

A tall man Faith remembered from Ray's Garage—what was his name? Oh yeah, Hank Lundegard—sauntered over to them. He came to a halt, his gaze sizing her up like a hungry man contemplating a T-bone.

A wave of heat rose up the side of Faith's neck.

"Why, you're lookin' as fresh and cool as a cup

o' vanilla ice cream, Miss Faith,'' Hank said with a lazy smile.

"Hank." Pastor Dan nodded his head, acknowledging the man, but a testiness had come into his voice. Faith looked at him in surprise. It was the first sign of coolness she'd heard mar that rich friendliness.

Hank ignored him.

"Would you like some more ice cream, Hank?"

The interloper tore his gaze from Faith and looked at the pastor. "No, thank you, Reverend. I done ate my fill of chocolate and strawberry."

He turned partly away from Dan and lowered his voice, speaking now to Faith alone. "I was just headin' over to the café." He smoothed his bushy mustache with one finger. "Care to come? We could have us a couple of brews. My treat."

Pastor Dan stepped forward. "Miss Richards has agreed to help me organize some youth activities, Hank."

Anger flared in Faith at his presumption. How dare he answer for her? And she hadn't agreed to help organize anything! She threw Dan a stare that clearly challenged his "little white lie." He didn't flinch, merely faced her down without blinking, as if he had every right in the world to make decisions for her.

She knew she was being foolish—more childish than Tami or Amy—but she just couldn't help it.

Impulsively she reached over and her fingers

curved around the eagle tattooed on Hank's arm. "Sure, Mr. Lundegard—uh, Hank. I don't drink, but a soda would be just great."

From the corner of her eyes, she saw Dan Whitman's face darken.

She forced a demure smile to her lips. "I'll see you later, Pastor. Please don't wait dinner for me. I may be a little late."

She sensed Dan's gaze boring into her back, and because of that, she added a gentle sway to her hips as she walked away from the ice cream social, on the arm of Hank Lundegard.

"Hey, little lady, how 'bout you and me going to my place?" Hank leaned across the small table and belched. His beer-laced breath turned her stomach upside down.

"Why would I want to go there?"

"So you and me could have ourselves a little party." He winked. "A little private party, if you know what I mean."

Faith winced at the pounding in her head and pulled her hand out from beneath his. She'd been foolish to come here. But not so foolish as to ever go home with him.

Truth to tell, she felt a little sheepish for going off with Hank Lundegard. A little sheepish? Faith grimaced. She was totally ashamed of herself. In fact, she'd spent the entire afternoon wanting to kick herself all around the block. Or Hank.

Why had she tried to tweak the good pastor that way? How childish!

Her "date," had turned out to be less than charming. Apparently believing that women like to be impressed, he'd dredged up any and all achievements from the time he'd entered grade school. She heard about the game-winning touchdown he'd scored in high school, his favorite kind of chewing tobacco and the huge assortment of Willow Hill girls whom he'd managed to bowl over. After two hours, she was ready to scream or make a polite, but hasty exit. She chose the latter.

"Hank, I'm so sorry. My head is splitting. I need to go to bed."

Hank's eyes lit up and he gave her body a raking gaze. "Nothin' to be sorry about, darlin'. I get them headaches, too."

Faith heaved a relieved sigh. "Then you understand...."

"Of course I do." His words slurred together, and for some reason Faith didn't feel reassured. "But I'm here to tell you this is your lucky day. Hank is going to give you a nice little massage, and when I'm through, I guarantee that headache of yours is going to be long gone. Then you and I can really have some fun."

Her heart skittered in alarm. She shifted uneasily in her chair and glanced around. They were alone in the cool dark interior. Everyone else, including the waitress, had gone outside to enjoy the outdoors.

Faith struggled to gather her thoughts. She'd heard you should never argue with a drunk, but she didn't have much choice. She searched for a way to tell him no, the pain medication and fatigue dulling her senses.

Apparently taking her hesitation for acquiescence, Hank smiled, gave her a cocky wink and pulled her to her feet. "C'mon, honey, let's not waste any more time."

Faith let out a little cry.

"Don't worry. Hank won't let you fall." He tightened his grip and drew her even closer. "You and me, we're going to be good together. I can tell."

Alarm rippled across her spine. "Let me go, Hank."

"Let me go, Hank." His voice mocked hers. "Honey, you don't have to play hard to get. We're both adults here, and if we want to have some fun, no one around here is going to care."

Fearful images of Hank's intentions swept like a wildfire through her mind, his words fanning the flame.

"Get your hands off me!" Her irate words were muffled by his lips closing over hers.

Her foot lashed out and grazed his shin. He chuckled as if she was playing some sort of childish game.

"I like to play rough, too," he whispered in her ear before he forced her head back and took her mouth again with a savage intensity.

"Let the lady go." A silken thread of warning ran through the unexpected voice.

Hank looked up at the interruption and his reddened eyes shifted toward the doorway.

"Why, Reverend Whitman, what a surprise. As you can see, I've got my hands full at the moment or I'd buy you a drink."

Pastor Dan's eyes gleamed in the dim light. "Hank, don't do this."

Hank heaved an irritated sigh. "Dan, I like you, but this is none of your concern. Go back and tend to your flock. This ewe is going home with me, whether you approve or not. Aren't you, sweetheart?"

"Dan…" Her voice trailed off helplessly.

"Let her go."

"Are you going to make me?" Hank said softly, mockingly.

"If I have to." An edge of steel ran through Dan's voice.

"What are you getting so riled about?" Hank laughed but his fingers loosened their hold. "She wants to go with me, don't you, honey?"

Faith was caught off guard by the conviction in his voice. For the first time, she realized the man had truly misread her intentions. Awkwardly she cleared her throat. "No, I don't."

Hank's brow furrowed and confusion warred with anger in his cloudy gaze. "Then why'd you tell me you did?"

"That doesn't matter. She doesn't want to go with you now." Dan moved steadily closer and gave Faith a quick smile of reassurance.

With one swift move, Hank released his hold and shoved her against the pastor. "There, take the little tease."

Faith cried out and would have fallen, but Dan reached out a steadying hand. Protectively his arms closed around her. "You did the right thing, Hank."

"Get her outta here."

For once Faith agreed with Hank's suggestion. She couldn't wait to go back to the parsonage and wash the stench of beer, smoke and Hank from her skin.

The cool night air outside the bar cleared her head. She didn't protest when Dan insisted they walk home. Faith wasn't sure if it was for her sake or his.

For all his calmness during the altercation with Hank, she'd sensed his underlying tension the moment she'd been flung into his arms. Once outside, Dan steadily increased his pace. The blocks came and went until finally Faith could stand the silence no more.

"It was stupid—" she said softly "—going with Hank."

Dan said nothing. His eyes focused firmly on the path ahead.

"I said I was sorry!" She spoke deliberately loud and this time she knew he'd heard.

He stopped so abruptly, she had to swerve to avoid crashing into him.

"I heard you the first time."

Faith lifted her chin. "Then why didn't you answer me?"

"I wasn't aware your comment required an answer."

"It most certainly did." Faith tossed her head, then stopped as she remembered she'd cut off her long curls last week. "I admit I made a mistake going with him—"

"You're right. Going with Hank was definitely a mistake. Not to mention, alcohol and medication can be a deadly combination."

"I'm not that stupid."

"Whatever."

"I didn't drink!"

Dan blew an exasperated breath, and for a moment he looked as though he wanted to throttle her. Instead, he inhaled deeply and reached over and took her hands in his. "You were a very lucky young woman tonight, Faith Richards. God was watching over you."

Faith jerked from his grasp and stood in the middle of the sidewalk, her hands clenched in fists at her side.

"God had nothing to do with it," she said, managing a look of cool disdain. "You helped me, not God."

He stood silent for a long moment. The air was so still, she might have thought he'd left, but for the light from the overhead moon shining down on him. "What would you say if I told you that I was already halfway home when I started back?"

"I'd say, you remembered something you'd forgotten—me!" she jeered.

"But I had forgotten, Faith. The afternoon was crazy. And then, when I did start home, my thoughts were focused on some changes I wanted to make in Sunday's sermon." He shook his head, "Until I heard a voice telling me to go to you."

"You want me to believe the heavens opened up and a great voice boomed instructions to you?" Faith forced a laugh. "Believe me, I'm much too inconsequential for God to be concerned with."

"God loves all his lambs, Faith. He cares what happens to you."

"Save your sermon for Sunday."

"Faith, I believe in a loving God."

"Go ahead. Believe in a winged cow for all I care."

"Faith—"

"Listen, I can't thank you enough for what you did for me back there. But you and I are worlds apart on what we believe. And that's something that's not going to change."

Faith glanced up with relief at the towering Victorian glowing in the moonlight. "Well, what do you know? We're home." She forced a smile to her trembling lips. "It's too bad it's so late. We'll have to continue our conversation some other time."

His jaw tightened and he opened his mouth. She braced herself for a sermon. Instead, Dan stared at her for a long moment. His gaze traveled over her face and searched her eyes.

The harsh uneven rhythm of his breathing resounded in her ears. Drops of moisture clung to his forehead. He softly brushed his fingers against her cheek. A strange languid heat filled her limbs. "Oh, Faith, I was really scared for you...."

"I'm so sorry I—"

The velvet warmth of his lips closing over hers smothered her last words. The sweet tenderness of the kiss took her breath away and she melted in his embrace.

"Thank God. I thank God he didn't hurt you," he whispered against her hair.

God. With one word the magic vanished. Faith stiffened.

He drew back immediately, regret lining his face. "Faith, I—"

She pressed her fingers firmly to his lips and shook her head. "It's time to say good-night. We're tired and it's been a really stressful day. For both of us."

Dan's eyes flickered, his expression solemn. "Of course."

She waited while he unlocked the door, resisting the urge to touch her still-tingling lips. Regardless of the convenient explanation she'd offered, she knew that what had just happened had very little to do with fatigue. Or stress. And a whole lot more with how Dan Whitman made her feel.

Chapter Four

"Faith." Dan pulled his bedroom door shut and hurried down the hall.

She turned slowly, her hand resting lightly on the newel. Short spikes of hair, still damp from the shower, framed her face. Her tight black jeans hugged her slim hips and her clingy purple shirt emphasized her curves. A watchful wariness filled her gaze.

For the past four days she'd left the parsonage at the crack of dawn, usually not returning until late at night. When their paths did cross, communication had been little more than verbal sparring. Though Aunt Dora had not said a word, Dan knew she'd felt the tension, too.

It was his fault. He accepted that. He'd been afraid for her and angry at Hank, but that still didn't explain why he'd done it. It still didn't explain why he'd kissed her.

Even though she wouldn't be in Willow Hill much longer, he had to make amends. He took a step forward. "About the other night—"

"Forget the sermon, Pastor." She held up her hands in mock surrender. "I already admitted going with Hank was a mistake."

Dan paused. Had this been why she'd been avoiding him? Because she expected a lecture on Hank? Didn't she realize he was far more worried about the effect of his own impulsive action?

As a minister, he'd always held himself to a higher standard of conduct. He'd violated that standard when he took her in his arms and kissed her. The fact that her spiritual life was in shambles made his action even more indefensible. How could he hope to minister to her soul if he couldn't seem to get past this disturbing awareness of the rest of her?

"I don't want to talk about Hank," he said curtly, the image of Hank's mouth on hers twisting like a knife in his chest. He forced himself back to the purpose of the conversation. "I want to talk about us."

"Us?" An impish smile lifted her lips and she raised one dark brow. "Funny, I don't recall there ever being an us."

"You know what I meant," Dan said, more sharply than he'd intended, jolted by the flicker of amusement in her green eyes.

A momentary flash of hurt crossed her face.

Dan stared at her in growing bewilderment and shame. He had misread her—he hadn't understood her teasing attempts to lighten a difficult situation.

"Say what you have to say," she said, crossing her arms in front of her and lifting her chin, her eyes cool and keen. "I'm in a hurry."

"I shouldn't have kissed you the other night." Dan raked his fingers through his hair. "It was wrong. Dead wrong. There was just something about you...."

"You're saying it's *my* fault you kissed me?" Her voice, though quiet, had an ominous quality. Two bright spots of color dotted her cheeks.

Dan frowned. She hadn't made him kiss her; he'd done it all on his own. "What I meant—"

She silenced him with a sweep of one hand, her violet-colored nails cutting a bright swath in the air. "Don't even bother. I know all too well what you meant."

"Faith—"

"I don't know why I even asked," she continued as if he hadn't even spoken. She raised her gaze to his and a strange light flickered in her eyes. "I guess I thought you were different."

Guilt for something he didn't even begin to understand swept through him. He opened his mouth, but before he could speak, she turned and headed down the stairs.

Dan followed and caught up with her on the landing. He grabbed her arm. "Wait one minute. Let me explain—"

She pulled from his grasp and stared at him, wide-eyed. "What is it you want from me?"

"I want..." He hesitated, the nearness of her driving the words he'd prepared from his head. The sweet scent of her perfume didn't help his concentration. Neither did the harsh uneven rhythm of her breathing.

Dan ignored the tiny pulse fluttering in her neck and the rich fullness of her lips and spoke slowly and deliberately so there could be no misunderstanding. "I want you to know how sorry I am about the other night. I shouldn't have kissed you. It was all my fault."

For a man who made his living with words, the heartfelt sentiment seemed even to his own ears woefully inadequate. Even so, a hint of a smile returned to Faith's lips.

"You really mean that?"

He nodded. Never had he meant anything more.

"I kissed you back," Faith admitted matter-of-factly. "So, if we're confessing, I'm afraid I'm just as guilty."

"It *had* been a long day," he said.

"And an even more stressful evening," Faith added.

"Friends?" Dan extended his hand.

"Friends."

He stared directly in her eyes and covered her

fingers in a warm grip. A sizzle of excitement raced up Faith's spine and her skin burned red-hot.

Stunned, Faith snatched her hand away. The force of the sudden move pushed her off balance. She teetered on the edge of the landing, her heart jumping high in her throat, her hands reaching for something solid to hold on to. She grabbed for Dan, her long nails raking his neck. He caught her arm, but the momentum carried him with her as they tumbled down the stairs. Dan bore the brunt of the impact, landing beneath her at the bottom.

Faith's heart thudded as if she'd just fallen from the top of a skyscraper instead of five short steps. Still, the hardwood floor was, well, hard, and Dan's lean muscular frame hadn't been much of a cushion. She shifted positions, pushing against him in an attempt to sit up.

Dan moaned.

Faith froze.

"Get off me!"

Faith immediately rolled off and scrambled to her feet. She glanced at Dan, surprised he continued to lie on his back, his knee now pulled to his chest.

"Are you okay?"

"Never better," he said, his voice laced with sarcasm.

Faith winced. Short claw marks traveled in thin red lines across the side of his neck, a finger's breadth apart.

She leaned over his supine figure for a closer look.

"I'm so sorry." She nervously brushed back a strand of hair. "I must have scratched you when I lost my balance. I certainly didn't mean—"

"Faith, can we talk about this later?"

She looked at him more closely, noticing for the first time the beads of sweat dotting his forehead.

"You're hurt," she said in surprise.

"My foot." He ground out the words through clenched teeth, his hands cradling an ankle that seemed to be swelling as she watched.

"Oh, my goodness." Faith's stomach churned. "I'll get Aunt Dora."

"She's not here."

"I'll call the paramedics." She headed for the phone.

"Don't. I'll be fine."

"It could be broken."

"No, I can move it." He grunted and flexed his toes. "It's only sprained."

"But you need help."

"You can help me."

Faith hesitated. She wouldn't be anyone's first choice for a nurse, not with her weak stomach and tendency to faint at the sight of blood. Still, he wasn't bleeding, and she *was* all he had. She took a deep breath and tried to remember what she'd learned in her basic first-aid class. Her eyes darted to the sofa in the parlor. "Wait a second."

A moment later Faith returned with a throw pillow. Moving quickly, she slipped off his shoe and tossed it to the side. She lifted Dan's ankle with both hands and elevated it on the soft mound. A shadow of pain crossed his face but he didn't complain.

"I'm sorry. I'm trying to be gentle."

"You're doing great." His smile seemed strained, but oddly his words made her feel better.

"I know something else that will help. I'll be right back."

Dan didn't argue. He just leaned against the bottom stair and closed his eyes.

Faith hurried to the kitchen and headed straight for the freezer. She threw open the door and reached for the ice cubes, but she'd used the last of them in her soda and had forgotten to refill the trays.

Her gaze scanned the racks and stopped on a sack of vegetables. It was one of her mother's old tricks. It would have to do.

"Faith, where are you?"

"Just a minute," she hollered, opening the corner cupboard and grabbing a couple of her pain pills. She filled a glass of water and hurried to the foyer.

"I've got peas—" she said, forcing a cheerful smile "—and I've got pills."

His eyes flickered over both objects. "I'm not even going to ask."

"We're out of ice, so that's why the peas and the pills will help your pain."

"This is all such a mess," he said, wiping a shaky hand across his forehead.

"Here, take these." She held out the caplets in one hand, the glass of water in the other.

"What are they?"

"The ones Doc Stewart gave me. They're super-mild."

"It won't matter. Pain pills knock me out."

His face, ashen and drawn, told her all she needed to know.

"You need something for the pain," she said firmly, using her best schoolteacher voice. "Take them."

To her surprise, he swallowed the pills without further argument. She smiled with satisfaction. Being a nurse wasn't as hard as she'd thought.

"Now, shut your eyes and relax," Faith said, molding the plastic bag of peas around his ankle.

His eyes snapped open at the coldness. She closed them with her fingers, feeling suddenly incredibly confident. "Give the pain pill and the peas—I mean the cold—a few minutes to work. When you're feeling better, we'll get you up in the chair."

Dan nodded wearily and his eyes drifted shut. Faith repositioned the bag and patted his hand reassuringly.

The scent of his rich warm musk mingled with her own light floral fragrance. Golden light spilled through the leaded glass of the front door. The world beyond the small foyer ceased to exist.

A firm believer in seizing the moment, Faith took full advantage of this unexpected opportunity. Her gaze drifted over Dan and she studied his features slowly, leisurely and for the first time, without interruption.

He was gorgeous, as beautiful as a Greek statue, shaped and molded to perfection. But Dan Whitman was not cold and lifeless. No, even at rest, he radiated a warmth and vitality that drew her to him.

It was just too bad he was a minister.

A strand of wheat-colored hair fell across his forehead and her fingers itched to see if the short curls were as soft as they looked.

A bolder woman might have touched. But Faith didn't dare. She had enough trouble eating just one M&M's. One touch might not be enough. Goodness knows, one kiss hadn't been.

Her heart sank at the red scratches on his neck.

"I'm so sorry, Dan," she whispered. One hand moved to his neck, the resolve to not touch forgotten.

Her finger traced the route of the battle scar she'd inflicted. She leaned over him, planning to drop one tiny kiss of apology along the wavery line's journey.

Her lips brushed his neck. Dan bolted upright and Faith tumbled back.

She scrambled to her feet, the heat rising up her

neck. Faith boldly met his gaze, her chin raised. "I was just inspecting your scratches."

If she just could have sustained that confident air, she might have convinced him.

By the time Aunt Dora returned from the church late that afternoon, Dan had been up and hobbling around for brief periods. The swelling had begun to subside. Swathed in an Ace bandage, his shoe may not have still fit, but he'd be able to get his baggy chinos off tonight. Thankfully the remnant of damage Faith's fingernails had inflicted were buried beneath a nutmeg-colored sweater she'd fetched earlier at his request.

"What happened to you?" Dora dropped her shawl on the settee and hurried across the room to where Dan now sat with his ankle propped up on a hassock.

Faith leaned against the mantel of the fireplace and took a long sip of her raspberry tea.

Dan cleared his throat. "I fell down the stairs."

"The stairs?" Dora blanched. "My dear boy, you're lucky to be alive. How did it happen?"

"I lost my balance on the landing," Dan said, casting Faith a pointed glance.

"Thank God Faith was here to help you."

A wry smile lifted Dan's lips. "Oh, she helped all right."

Keenly aware of his scrutiny, Faith focused her

gaze on the crackling fire and tried to control the heat creeping up her neck.

Aunt Dora's eyes narrowed, her speculative gaze shifting between Faith and Dan. A smile creased the wrinkled lips. "It looks like you two accomplished a lot today."

"Not really," Faith said, wondering just what it was, if anything, they'd accomplished today. Her questioning gaze locked on Dan's face, but he only shrugged. "Dan's been in the chair most of the day and I've just been keeping him company."

"Faith even canceled her appointment to get her nails done so she could play nursemaid," Dan said. A twinkle sparkled in his eye.

Faith heaved a long-suffering sigh. "It was indeed a sacrifice, but I couldn't leave the poor cripple to fend for himself."

Dan chuckled and she couldn't help but smile back. Actually, the afternoon had been quite... nice. They'd talked, played checkers on the board Dan had gotten for his tenth birthday and snacked on goldfish crackers. It had been years since she'd eaten so many of the tiny crackers or laughed so much. Once they'd determined the kiss had simply been a mistake, they'd felt free to enjoy each other's company.

A satisfied light shone in Dora's eyes. "Harold called for you over at the church today. He wants you to bring out last Sunday's church bulletin when you stop by tomorrow."

Dan winced and shifted in his chair. "The way this ankle feels now, I'm not sure I'll be able to even make it this week, much less tomorrow. I certainly don't think I'm up to driving a stick shift."

"Ah, yes, the ankle." A thoughtful gaze crossed Aunt Dora's face. "I'd drive you myself, but I'm hosting the Ladies' Circle here tomorrow."

Ladies' Circle.

Faith cringed. She'd grown used to Aunt Dora's nosy meddling but the thought of a whole roomful of such women sent her stomach churning with anxiety and dread.

"I can drive him," Faith said quickly.

Dan's eyebrows slanted upward.

"I couldn't ask you to do that," he said, flashing her an insincere smile.

"You didn't ask, I volunteered." She ignored the warning in his eyes. They'd both agreed this afternoon it would be best to keep their distance, but she'd have to make an exception in this instance.

"Faith, I know the shut-ins will thank you." Aunt Dora nodded in approval.

"The truck's a stick," Dan said.

"Pastor Dan," Dora said in an exasperated tone, "if Faith knows how to drive a motorbike, I'm sure she knows how to shift."

His gaze captured hers. "Is that right?"

Faith swallowed past the lump caught in her throat and nodded. After all, how hard could it be?

* * *

The truck lurched forward in one final effort, the spasmodic jerk carrying it into the farmyard. Faith stole a glance at Dan. Same stony expression.

It hadn't taken long before Faith's lack of prowess in handling a manual transmission became apparent. She'd killed the engine four times before leaving the driveway. A lesser man might have cursed.

But Dan had not spoken other than to give her a few pearls of automotive wisdom, such as "Let the clutch out slowly while giving it gas," and "Put in the clutch *before* you shift."

Thankfully, she'd been so focused on conquering a standard transmission, the miles to Harold's farm had flown, despite the uncomfortable silence.

"We're here."

"So we are."

"I'll help you inside." Faith kept her voice brisk and businesslike. If he could be cold, she could be downright icy. "Then I'll wait for you in the truck."

"You will not," he said, pushing his door open.

She gritted her teeth, fully prepared to tell him she'd do as she pleased, thank you very much, when the stubborn man started to ease himself out of the pickup.

A lesser woman might have let him fall and break his neck. But he'd come to her rescue before. She could do no less for him.

Faith scrambled out the driver's side and rounded

the truck in a flash, making a lunging grab as he started to fall.

"You're a fool," she whispered in his ear.

"Not so foolish," he grunted as he righted himself. "I knew you'd be there."

She glanced sideways just in time to catch the twinkle in his eyes and the grin playing at the corners of his lips.

Only the thought of how it would look to the elderly man now standing on the porch, staring with interest at the unexpected excitement, stopped Faith's elbow from jabbing Dan squarely in his ribs.

"Ready?" His breath, warm against her cheek, drove the remaining thoughts of violence from her head. The unwelcome temptation to turn her face and bring those lips within reach took her by surprise.

Faith gritted her teeth and forced her gaze back to the farmyard, searching for obstacles that might impede their journey to the front porch.

"Let's go." She secured his arm firmly in hers. His muscular arm tightened beneath the wool sweater and she shivered in response.

"Are you cold?" Dan's gaze shifted and lingered on her thin sweater.

She'd pulled on the silver-gray cashmere cardigan this morning, not for its warmth or practicality but because she liked the way it looked with her black twill pants. If the look burning in his eyes was any indication, Dan liked it too.

"Actually, I'm—" she briefly considered being honest and saying "hot," which is what she was, but decided to play it safe "—comfortable."

His left eyebrow rose a fraction but he just shrugged. "If you say so."

They'd barely started toward the house when Dan stopped abruptly. Faith lurched forward, almost losing her balance and him in the process.

"What the—"

"My Bible," he said with an apologetic smile. "I left it in the truck."

Bible. Faith groaned under her breath.

"I'll get it." She helped him over to the gate of the white picket fence that encircled the tiny front yard. Satisfied that he wouldn't topple over, she returned to the pickup.

Faith jerked the door open and reached across the vinyl seat. Her fingers closed around the soft black leather. An icy chill traveled up her spine.

Coming with him today had been a mistake. A gaggle of cackling hens—or for that matter, a pack of rabid dogs—would pose less of a threat than this handsome minister.

It didn't matter that his eyes were as blue as the Midwestern sky or that his quick wit made her laugh. It only made him more dangerous to her heart and ultimately—to her soul.

Chapter Five

Faith paced up and down the shiny linoleum aisles of the A & P frantically trying to recall what it was she'd come to pick up. Why couldn't she remember? If only she had a list.

She stopped in her tracks and breathed a sigh of relief. Why had she wasted so much time? She always made a list before going to the store. Faith opened her purse and shoved aside her breath mints, comb and a packet of tissues, searching for that essential scrap of paper.

Her eyes widened. She jerked the sides of the bag open farther, nearly tearing the seams. She leaned closer. Her mind reeled. How could it be?

Faith gritted her teeth, and before she could chicken out, she shoved her hand into the bag. Her fingers curved around soft leather and her heart flip-flopped. She pulled the object out into the bright fluorescent light.

She held the book out in front of her, a sinking feeling crowding the pit of her stomach. With a nail she traced the name embedded in gold on the front cover—Daniel Whitman. A chill traveled up her spine.

How had his Bible gotten in her purse? It was much too big to have just dropped into the bag accidentally. What explanation could there be? Dora wouldn't have placed it there; she knew how often Dan used his Bible, how often he referenced God's word.

God's word?

Dan might consider it God's word. Dora might consider it God's word. But to Faith it was a book, like *War and Peace* or *Pride and Prejudice,* a great literary work, no more no less. Faith dropped the Bible back into her bag and rested one hand on a half-empty shelf, suddenly feeling light-headed. Maybe she was coming down with something. Or maybe the stress was finally catching up with her.

The Faith that everyone saw had handled the events of the last year with amazing aplomb. On the inside the need to maintain control had taken its toll. The false charges. Losing her job. The plane crash. The endless days of waiting until her parents had been declared dead.

Would it have been easier if their bodies had been found? She brushed the thought aside, knowing deep in her heart nothing could have made those horrible days and weeks after the plane crash any easier.

"Turn your sorrows over to the Lord," had been her uncle George's suggestion. He'd meant well and she'd been too far into her grief to even argue with him, to tell him there was no one, not even a God she no longer believed in who had the power to comfort her. Only having her parents back would help, and that was impossible.

She caught sight of a red sweater coat with white piping at the far end of the aisle. Her mother had a coat just like that. She'd given it to her on her last birthday.

Faith blinked back the moisture and wiped a shaky hand across her brow. She hadn't been this emotional since she'd first learned of her uncle's heart problems. What had brought this on?

Harold.

This had all begun when she'd gone with Dan to visit Harold. The man had spent almost the entire time talking about how lonely he'd been since his wife had died. He'd brought up several times how he'd see someone and say to himself, "I need to tell Ethel what they're up to," only to realize Ethel wasn't there and no one else would care.

Faith could empathize. There'd been so many times she'd started to pick up the phone to call her mother, so many times she'd hung up without dialing.

That must be it, she decided. Harold's remembrances had stirred up her own memories, and Dan's religious comments had been just enough to arouse her emotions. Emotions that had been held quite nicely in check until Dan had started in with his God talk.

Faith squared her shoulders, determined not to waste any more energy on pointless emotions. She'd concentrate her efforts instead on marching down every aisle of the store until she remembered why she was here, then she'd go home to bed and put this all behind her.

She rounded the corner of the aisle and stopped dead in her tracks. A blonde wearing the red coat stood by the dairy case, laughing with a tall dark-haired man. The woman's hand rested on his arm in a gesture so familiar it took Faith's breath away.

"Mom? Dad?" Her voice shook so bad, it would be a miracle if they heard her.

But she must have been louder than she thought because they immediately turned and smiled. Joy sluiced through every inch of her body.

Dear God, it had been a mistake. They hadn't died. They'd found where she was and had come to get her.

Tears streamed down her face. At this moment, she wanted nothing more than to feel their arms around her, to smell her father's spicy cologne and the lavender scent her mother had worn for as long as Faith could remember, but her legs refused to cooperate. Like posts mired in concrete, no matter how much she tried, she couldn't get them to move an inch.

But couldn't they come to her? They'd heard her call and they'd recognized her. She was sure of it.

"Mom. Dad. It's me, Faith." She opened her arms, already anticipating how good it would feel to be wrapped in their embrace.

Her anticipation quickly turned to horror. Instead of coming toward her, her mother said something to her father and they started to walk away!

"Don't go!" Panic clawed at her throat. She wouldn't let them leave her. "Please don't leave me."

They headed for the door, and suddenly Faith knew if they left now she wouldn't ever see them again.

"No!" her voice cracked.

They took another step, her mother casting a regret-filled glance over her shoulder.

"No!" her voice rose.

The A & P's automatic door opened.

"No—" she cried at the top of her lungs, despair overtaking her.

"Faith. Wake up. You're having a nightmare."

Firm gentle hands shook her shoulders. Her eyes popped open. Her heart pounded as if she'd just run a long race. Frantically her gaze searched the room.

Dan's hand gently took her face and turned it

toward his. "Take a deep breath and tell me what's wrong? What's got you so upset?"

His voice was low and soothing and his eyes were filled with concern.

"I saw them," she said, her mind a crazy mixture of hope and fear. "At the A & P."

Dan's brows drew together. "Who did you see?"

"My mom and dad. By the dairy case." Her lips trembled and her eyes filled with fresh tears.

"Your parents are in Willow Hill?" Confusion clouded his gaze. "I thought your parents were dead."

"They are." With the words a heaviness settled in her chest, an understanding of what had occurred. She swallowed with difficulty and found her voice. "They weren't there, were they?"

Dan handed her a tissue from the bedside table and shook his head.

She dabbed her eyes, swallowing the sob that rose as her hopes sank.

"I'm so sorry." Dan pulled her close and pressed her head to his chest, the terry cloth of his robe soft against her cheek. "It was just a dream. A nightmare."

"I was so happy to see them." She sniffed. "I wanted so much for it to be true."

"I can see that," he said softly, one hand stroking her hair.

Faith listened to his heart's steady beat and took comfort in his strength, no longer feeling so alone.

"Daniel?" Aunt Dora stood in the doorway, her hair set in black brush rollers and covered with a hair net, her silk robe with brightly covered flowers cinched tight around her waist.

Faith lifted her head and brushed back the tear-dampened hair from her face, conscious for the first time that she wore nothing but a skimpy cotton nightgown.

Dan gave Faith a reassuring smile and rose awkwardly. "Faith had a nightmare."

"My dear, are you okay?" Dora bustled across the room and took Dan's seat at the edge of the bed. Her expression filled with concern.

"I saw my parents." It was all she could do not to burst into disappointed tears. "I wanted to hug them, but I couldn't get close enough."

"She thought she saw them at the A & P," Dan said, shooting Dora a worried look.

"Have your parents passed on?" Dora asked softly.

Faith nodded, trying to swallow past the lump in her throat.

"Dan, why don't you go down and make us all some hot tea?" Dora gestured with her head toward the door.

"Will you be okay?" Dan cast a questioning glance at Faith.

Dora took Faith's hand and patted it. "We'll be just fine, won't we, honey?"

Faith nodded, suddenly incredibly weary. The lie

she'd been telling herself for the last year passed easily from her lips. "I'm just fine."

Dan headed downstairs to brew the tea. The water had just started to boil when Dora came into the kitchen. Alone.

"How is she?"

Dora smiled wearily and sat down. "She's sleeping now. Poor thing, that nightmare really took it out of her."

"I didn't quite understand," Dan said. "Her parents are dead but she dreamed she saw them at the A & P?"

The older woman studied him for a long minute. "You've never lost anyone you've loved, have you?"

Dan hesitated then shook his head. "Not really. My aunt Lucy died last year but she'd always lived in California so I can't say that I knew her that well."

Dora sipped her tea. "Then it is probably difficult for you to fully understand how devastating the death of a loved one can be. Many people dream about those they've lost. Faith's type of dream is actually fairly common."

"But at the A & P?"

Dora chuckled. "I had a similar experience to Faith's, except in my dream Herbert was slopping the hogs. I'm sure given the choice he would have preferred I'd seen him in that ratty old recliner he loved."

"I felt so helpless," Dan said. "I wanted to comfort her, but I didn't know how."

"It looked to me like you were doing okay," Dora said dryly.

Dan could feel the warmth rise up his neck. He wished he could drop this subject but he couldn't with Faith's reputation at stake.

"Dora." His voice cracked. He took a deep breath, feeling all of fifteen again. "We need to be clear on one thing. I only went into Faith's bedroom because I heard her scream. Nothing happened."

"You're a dear boy, Dan." The old woman leaned across the table and patted his hand. "I understand what you're saying."

"Good," he said. "That's settled then."

"Not so fast." Dora's gaze grew thoughtful. "I'm not so old or so naive that I can't pick up on the chemistry between you two."

Dan opened his mouth to protest, but Dora raised one hand. "Be careful. That's all I'm saying."

He forced a chuckle. "Dora, take my word for it. You don't have a thing to worry about."

He and Faith Richards? Dan picked up his cup and shook his head. Not in a million years.

Chapter Six

"I don't have a clue what I'm going to do today." Faith propped her elbow on the kitchen table and watched Aunt Dora pour chocolate batter into a heart-shaped cake pan.

The older woman looked up momentarily. "You could help me make cakes for the church bazaar."

"I think I'll pass." She couldn't believe Dora would even offer. The last time she'd assisted the woman with cooking they'd both been crazy by the time the food was on the table. Dora believed in a dash of this, a pinch of that and maybe a smidgen of something else, whereas Faith had to precisely weigh and measure absolutely everything.

"Good afternoon, ladies." Dressed casually in jeans and a long-sleeved denim shirt, Dan sauntered into the room.

Faith sighed. The man was way too gorgeous to be a minister. Whoever said life wasn't fair sure hadn't been kidding.

Dan headed straight to the refrigerator. He opened the door and stared into the cool recesses, finally pulling out a soda. "Don't hold dinner. I'm not sure I'll be back in time."

Dora clucked disapprovingly at the bright red can in his hand. "At least let me get you a proper lunch. It'll take just a minute to fix you a nice roast beef sandwich and a glass of milk."

"I'm not hungry," Dan said.

"You not hungry? The man who wants a snack an hour after a big meal? I don't believe it." Faith searched his face, but her untrained eye could find no sign of alien possession. He *looked* like the same old Dan.

He shrugged and opened the soda.

"I almost forgot." Dora's expression softened. "This afternoon's the farm sale."

Dan nodded. He met the older woman's thoughtful gaze, and a wordless moment of understanding seemed to pass between them. "Yep, today's the day."

Farm sale? Faith's ears perked up. Although she didn't have much extra money, the event certainly sounded like more fun than her two other options: watching the grass grow or helping Dora bake cakes.

"I'm ready." Faith stood and tossed her napkin on the table.

Dan shook his head. "I don't think that's a good idea."

"Why not?" She made no effort to keep the irritation from her voice.

"Dan," Dora said suddenly, "let her go."

"Thank you, Dora." Faith flashed the woman a grateful smile.

Dan's lips tightened and his jaw set in that stubborn tilt she'd started to become intimately acquainted with. "I don't think—"

"Dan," Dora said more firmly this time. "Take her with you."

His gaze lifted questioningly to the older woman's.

"Hel-lo," Faith said, not liking being talked about as if she wasn't there. "Anyone want to tell me what's going on here?"

Dan's gaze returned to Dora's. He heaved a resigned sigh and gestured to Faith. "Let's go."

Although not quite sure what had brought about this abrupt turnaround, Faith was determined not to look a gift horse in the mouth. She smiled happily at Dora and grabbed her purse, unable to resist a little teasing. She batted her lashes at Dan. "Decided it would be more fun if I came along?"

Dan's lips tipped in a slight smile. He opened the back door and waved her through. "Something like that."

They took the truck and Faith chattered all the way, enjoying the change of scenery and paying no attention to Dan's unusual silence.

The drive went quickly and when Dan turned off the county road onto a long winding drive, Faith scooted to the edge of her seat. She'd always loved a good shopping trip and if this ancient farmstead wasn't exactly Nordstrom, it would have to do.

The neglected farm lane was deeply rutted. Dan drove slowly, steering back and forth in an attempt to avoid the deepest of the chuckholes. They'd almost reached the end of the drive when suddenly one wheel dropped into a hole the size of the Grand Canyon. The truck jolted and Faith flew across the seat.

Dan reached out instinctively. Embarrassed at slamming into him, Faith could only laugh.

He wheeled the pickup into the nearest parking place and Faith brushed her hair back from her face.

"Well, well, what have we here?" Hank Lundegard reclined against a shiny red 4x4, the infuriating grin Faith remembered from Rockwell's Café plastered across his face.

Faith straightened and scooted back to her own side of the seat.

"Great," Dan muttered under his breath. He turned off the engine and pulled the keys from the ignition without once glancing in Faith's direction.

"Glad to see you could make the sale,

Preacher,'' Hank said. "And it's always good to see your little roommate."

Dan jerked open the door, almost hitting Hank in the process. "How you doing, Hank?"

Hank shot a wad of chewing tobacco out the side of his mouth, missing Dan's shoes by only inches. "Purty good."

Faith slid out the door, careful to watch her step. Hank's face brightened and he flashed her an appreciative smile. "Miss Faith, you shore do look nice."

She glanced down at the outfit she'd dug out of the drawer this morning. The black sueded fleece pants were coupled with a short-sleeved gray-and-black cotton shirt. Granted, the outfit was stylish but hardly one expected to garner such wolfish looks. "Thanks."

The man continued to stare expectantly. He looked different today, cleaner and well kept. His T-shirt was obviously new, and although his jeans were worn, they weren't frayed. Even the big silver buckle on his belt gleamed.

Faith hesitated. Was he waiting for her to return the compliment? "You look...nice, too."

Hank's grin widened and he elbowed his buddy next to him. Faith wished she'd kept her mouth shut.

She brushed past him with a cursory smile and Dan followed behind. The narrow aisle wasn't wide enough for them to walk side by side between all the vehicles parked in long rows on the green lawn. The once-lush grass was now flat and lifeless.

Faith swore the entire population of Willow Hill must have turned out for the sale, and every single person seemed determined to visit with the pastor. They'd go a few feet only to stop again. By the time they finally reached the main yard, not only had the word *pastor* started to grate on her nerves, but the blue sky had turned gray.

The forecast had been for unseasonably warm temperatures but the unpredictable Nebraska climate had not cooperated. A gust of wind swept across the flat fields and Faith shivered, the light cotton shirt not much protection against the brisk north breeze.

Dan had been the smart one, she thought, staring longingly at his hooded sweatshirt.

"C'mon, let's look over there."

Dan's hand cupped her back. Faith shivered again, but this time she couldn't blame the weather.

Dan paused and his gaze dropped, lingering on the goose bumps dotting her bare arms. Before she could say a word, he shrugged off his sweatshirt and draped it around her shoulders.

"I can't take—"

"Keep it," he said. "I'm not cold at all."

"Thanks. I was..." Faith's voice trailed off and stopped.

Dan's attention had shifted to a mid-thirties couple standing down by an empty corral. Two lines appeared between his eyes. He gave Faith's shoulder an absentminded squeeze. "I'll be back."

"Hey," she said. "You didn't tell me how I bid."

Always a survivor, Faith scouted around until she found the registration area. She got her number and headed straight for the table that had caught her eye on their way in, the one positively overflowing with junk.

Drawn to the jewelry, Faith picked through the assorted brooches, earrings and necklaces thrown together in an open box before her gaze shifted to a locked glass case holding the finer pieces.

Immediately, an emerald-cut ruby ring surrounded by tiny diamonds caught her eye. Ruby was her birthstone and she'd always been partial to any jewelry made with the sparkling red gem.

Faith leaned closer for a better look. She straightened after only a second and glanced around. The freckled redhead who'd been down by the corral now stood behind her.

The woman continued to stare and Faith's face warmed. She cleared her throat, pretending to be unaffected.

"Have you seen it?" She gestured to the case. "I was just looking at the ruby ring. It's gorgeous."

"My husband gave it to me for our first anniversary." A tiny muscle flickered in the woman's jaw.

"This is *your* sale?"

The woman nodded and extended her hand. "I'm Sue Perry. Pastor Dan suggested I come over and introduce myself."

"I'm glad you did." Faith shook her hand and glanced around the yard. "By the way, where is Dan?"

Sue gestured toward the white clapboard farmhouse. "He and John, my husband—" she added in answer to Faith's blank stare "—went up to the house. The girls are at their grandparents so it should be quiet."

Faith nodded as if she understood, but she didn't have a clue. She had no idea why the woman had been gazing at her with such a pensive expression or why Sue's husband was up talking to a minister. Actually, she preferred to stay out of whatever was going on.

"I really do like that ring," Faith said.

"Then you should bid on it," Sue said, picking at a cuticle.

"I might." Faith cast another glance at the display case. "If you don't mind my asking, why are you selling it?"

To her chagrin, Sue's eyes filled with tears.

"Hey, I didn't mean—"

"No, it's not you." Sue blinked back the moisture and took a deep breath. "Look, Dan thought you might like to join us up at the house?"

And listen to Dan spout his religious babble? No way. Faith picked up a silver chain from the junk pile and twisted it between her fingers. "Thanks for the invitation, but if you don't mind, I think I'll just stay and browse for a while."

A startled expression flitted across Sue's freckled face. "Certainly."

Without another word Sue turned and headed back up the hill toward the house, her shoulders stiff.

Faith watched her for a moment then turned her attention back to the jewelry.

In the end, she only bought the ring. It went higher than she'd wanted but for some reason she couldn't let it go to the steely-eyed man with the sour expression.

By the time the auctioneer had finished with the household items and had moved on to the tools and farm equipment, Faith had lost interest.

She collected the ring, virtually wiping out her meager savings in the process.

"What a beautiful setting." The auctioneer's assistant, an attractive girl with her dark hair pulled back in a ponytail, cast an admiring glance at the glittering stone.

Faith nodded, still unable to understand how anyone could bear to part with such a ring. "I can't believe she'd sell it."

The girl lowered her voice. "The way I hear it, I don't think she had much choice."

"Really?" Faith said. "Why?"

"I don't like to gossip." The woman's gaze

darted around the empty garage as if to make sure she wouldn't be overheard. "Word is John insisted everything be sold. Supposedly he's promised he'll pay everyone back in full, even though he wouldn't need to do that, what with the bankruptcy and—"

"Bankruptcy," Faith said loudly. "They're filing bankruptcy?"

"Shh." The brunette frowned. "Not so loud. They didn't want to file, but I guess they didn't have much choice."

"What happened?"

The girl thought for a moment. "Some of it you can blame on the weather. Some on the equipment John inherited from his father. It was old and needed a lot of work. Some on the falling prices. Actually it seemed everything that could go wrong did. It's very sad. John and Sue are hard workers, but they just got further and further behind."

In a daze Faith wandered out of the garage, a sick feeling in the pit of her stomach. Dora and Dan's conversation now made sense.

She shoved the ring into her pocket and quickly crossed the farmyard. The crowd had thinned and only some die-hard old-timers dressed predominantly in overalls and seed caps remained, hovering about the tools.

Faith slipped past the group, breathing a sigh of relief when she didn't encounter Hank's hulking form. She'd been lucky today. She hadn't seen him since he'd celebrated his winning bid on a case of limited-edition Billy Beer cans with a big war whoop.

As much as she disliked the man, the memory made her smile.

Faith zipped Dan's sweatshirt all the way up and headed toward the house, the musky scent of his cologne embracing her skin from all sides.

The closer she got to the house, the more her feet slowed. Would Sue be angry when she found out Faith had bought her ring? Taking a deep breath, Faith climbed the rickety wooden steps to the front porch. The sound of voices drew her gaze. The curtains were pulled back and the window open. Dan and a man she assumed to be John stood in the living room. By the look on Sue's husband's face, he was definitely angry.

"Can I get you some coffee? Or maybe a pop?"

Faith jumped, her heart lodging in her throat. Half-hidden in the dusky shadows, Sue Perry sat in the swing, an afghan of brown and orange squares draped over her lap.

"No thanks." Faith shot another quick glance into the living room. Cold as it was outside, the porch still seemed the better choice. "Can I join you?"

"Sure. I'd like that." Sue patted the seat beside her and in the light she looked much too young to be anyone's mother and much too sweet to have to endure such hardship.

Faith took the seat next to Sue. For several long

moments neither of them spoke and Faith struggled to frame an apology.

"I'm sorry," she said finally.

"For what?" Sue asked in surprise.

"I thought this was just a big garage sale." Faith rolled the cord of the sweatshirt between her fingers. "I didn't realize this wasn't a voluntary thing."

Sue nodded, accepting the apology without question. "Don't give it another thought. I'm just glad it's almost over. The last couple of weeks have been so horrible, it's got to get better."

The young woman's voice broke and she dropped her gaze.

Faith reached out and gave Sue's hand a comforting squeeze. "It'll be okay."

"Sure it will." Sue straightened and wiped the tears from her eyes with the tips of her fingers. "I told John we have a lot to be thankful for. We still have each other, and God has blessed us in so many ways. We're healthy, we have three beautiful daughters…"

The woman rattled on and Faith wondered who she was trying to convince—herself or Faith. If she was trying to convince Faith, she might as well stop now. She didn't have a prayer. The Lord had blessed them indeed!

It was all Faith could do not to tell Sue to wake up and smell the coffee. This young couple had been left in the lurch just as Faith had once been.

Forsaken by a God who'd promised never to forsake.

Promises. Faith snorted.

"Thanks for listening, Faith," Sue said finally. "I can see why Dan likes you."

Faith returned the woman's smile without comment. Obviously God wasn't the only thing the woman was mistaken about.

Talking had seemed to ease Sue's burden, and the two women sat side by side in the swing in a comfortable silence. The swing slowly moved back and forth and fireflies appeared out of nowhere to dot the now-empty yard with their momentary flashes of light.

"Frankly, Pastor, I don't feel like praying." John Perry's angry voice wafted through the open window, the lace curtains blowing in the breeze.

Faith cocked her head and listened, intently pleased that someone else was as realistic as she was.

She stole a quick glance at Sue. The woman's lips tightened and her gaze remained fixed straight ahead on the setting sun.

"John." Dan's soothing voice resounded in the stillness, but the man cut him short immediately.

"Pastor, I don't want to argue with you. I've called out to the Almighty until I'm blue in the face, and I still lost my land," John said, spacing the words evenly. "This farm has been in my family for four generations."

The pain in the man's voice was unmistakable, and Faith's heart ached in sympathy. She knew the anguish that came with losing something you loved.

"Four generations, that's a long time," Dan said. "Didn't I hear from someone that your great-grandfather settled here back in the 1870s?"

Faith shook her head in disbelief. How could he bring up the past? She held her breath and waited for John to blast the minister's insensitivity.

"That's right," John said, his voice surprisingly losing some of its steely edge. "He and my great-grandmother left Ohio and came out here with nothing. They fell in love with this part of the country and never went any farther."

"So he built a house, planted crops and—" a smile sounded in Dan's voice "—started to raise children."

"You've apparently heard the story." John laughed. "Most folks around here who are familiar with the Perrys say great-granddad's best crop was his twenty kids."

Twenty! Faith stifled a gasp.

Dan chuckled. "Sounds like he took the Lord seriously when he said to be fruitful and multiply."

"I never thought about it quite that way." John popped the top off a can of soda and took a sip.

"Your grandfather took it over in what? The twenties?"

"Yes, 1929, right when the Depression hit. But no matter how bad things got, he managed to hang on to the land.'' Bitterness spilled back into John's words and Sue tensed beside her.

Faith leaned back against the swing and let her mind wander. She deliberately blocked out the voices inside the house. Dusk shifted to dark and the halogen lamp standing tall near the garage turned on, casting an apron of light throughout the yard. The last of the vehicles pulled away with its truck bed heaped to the brim.

''Looks like the sale's over,'' Faith said softly, glancing at Sue.

Sue shook her head and placed a finger to her lips, her ear cocked in the direction of the window.

Dan's rich baritone resounded in the stillness. ''It's easy to forget that God is what matters, not the land. God is the only constant. The land will one day be gone, but God will always be there for us. He's what we need to focus on, not earthly matters.''

''I guess it makes sense.''

''You can't lose something that was never really yours to lose.''

''Because it was always God's.''

''Exactly,'' Dan said.

''I don't mind telling you, Pastor, I've been pretty low lately,'' John said. ''But what you said…well, it makes sense. And in a weird sort of way it does make me feel better. I think I might even be able to sleep tonight.''

Sue moved beside her and Faith turned just in time to see two tears slide down Sue's face.

"Are you okay?" Faith said so softly, her lips barely moved.

"I've been so worried about him." Sue dabbed at her tears with a wadded-up tissue. "He's felt so guilty, like such a failure. I was afraid of what he might do."

Faith patted Sue's hand, wondering why she had ever thought this day would be fun.

"John isn't the only one who'll sleep tonight. But before I fall asleep I'm going to make sure I thank God."

"Thank God?"

"For all his blessings. And," Sue added, her gaze shifting to stare at the two men in the living room, "for sending us Pastor Dan."

"Want to stop for ice cream?" Dan shot a quick glance at Faith. He'd tried to make conversation a few times since they'd left the Perry farm, but she hadn't responded much past yes or no.

She gave a noncommittal shrug. "Doesn't matter to me. Whatever you want to do."

"I say yes." Dan turned at the next street and headed toward Willow Hill's business district.

In a matter of minutes he'd pulled up in front of a tiny frame building that looked like it might have once been someone's garage. Blistered and peeling, its ancient white siding stood in stark contrast to the clean and shiny windows and the obviously new flashing cone on the rooftop.

Dan shut off the engine and hopped out, hesitating when Faith stayed seated.

"I'll wait here," she said, her gaze fixed on Johnson Hardware's preseason display of snow-blowers.

"No way," Dan said. Without another word, he rounded the front of the pickup and threw open her door. "You're keeping me company."

Faith's brow lifted.

"C'mon, trust me." He shot her an enticing smile. "A lime slush and a hot fudge sundae is good for whatever ails you."

Her lips twitched. "If that were true, we'd all weigh three hundred pounds and not have a care in the world."

"Give it a try." He took her arm, not giving her a chance to protest further. "They use real whipped cream."

Faith heaved an irritated sigh but she knew she didn't stand a chance when Dan Whitman turned on his charm. "All right, but if I don't fit on that Harley when it's time for me to blow this popsicle stand, I'm holding you personally responsible."

He laughed, and by the time they reached the counter, he had her laughing, too.

Dan shoved his hand into his pocket and pulled out three crumpled bills and assorted change. "Order what you want," he said, glancing down at the money in his palm. "As long as it doesn't cost more than three dollars and fifty-three cents."

"Pastor Dan." The smile on the face of the girl behind the counter widened at the sight of the pastor. It faded when it shifted to Faith.

"Lisa." Dan smiled. "I didn't know you worked here."

"I just started last week," she said.

Faith pretended to study the menu. Despite what Dan had said about a hot fudge sundae, a root beer float or a malt was more her speed.

"Have you met Faith yet?"

Faith stifled a groan. Why did the man feel he had to introduce her to everyone?

"No." Lisa shook her head. "I haven't."

"Faith Richards, this is Lisa Lundegard. Lisa is Hank's daughter."

Faith glanced up just in time to see a red flush creep up the girl's neck. A flash of sympathy for what the girl must have to endure with such a father made Faith's smile especially warm. "Lisa, it's nice to meet you."

"You, too." The girl dropped her gaze.

Faith took a deep breath and gave it one more shot. "I used to work in a dairy sweet shop when I was about your age."

"You did?" Lisa looked up, and this time her smile was genuine.

"Until they fired me," Faith said ruefully.

Lisa's eyes widened. "Why?"

Faith placed her elbows on the counter and leaned forward conspiratorially. "Making the cones too big."

"I hardly think they'd fire you for giving some-one too much ice cream," Dan said, his expression clearly disbelieving.

"You didn't know Mr. Bomberger, the manager. He insisted we weigh practically everything. To this day I have a hard time not weighing and measuring." Faith laughed. "I think the man scarred me for life."

"Our manager's like that, too. Our small cones can't be more than five ounces or—" Lisa raised a finger and pretended to slice her throat.

"Speaking of manager," Dan said in a low voice, "I believe he wants us to order."

Faith glanced sideways. The beady-eyed man with the sour expression that had bid against her at the auction stood back by the grill, his lips pursed together giving them a prunelike appearance.

"I think you're right," she said to Dan. Then, in a voice loud enough to carry to the back, she said, "Thanks, Lisa, for taking the time to let me know all my options on those malts. I think I will have the chocolate chip."

Lisa flashed her a grateful smile.

Dan, for all his talk, ended up with just a small chocolate cone.

"I hope this isn't more than five ounces," he teased as Lisa handed him the cone. His blue eyes sparkled good-naturedly and dimples flashed in both cheeks. Lisa giggled. Faith could see why all the women liked him.

Faith confiscated a straw for her malt and Dan plucked a couple of napkins from the shiny metal dispenser on the counter. They bid Lisa goodbye and headed to one of the weathered picnic tables at the side of the building. Faith could feel the curious glances they were attracting, and she wondered if she should mention to Dan that being seen out with her on Friday night might not be such a good idea.

"You didn't have to pay for me," she said, knowing that hadn't escaped the notice of many of his parishioners in line behind them. "I have money."

"I thought you spent your wad on that ruby ring." He licked the perimeter of the cone and wiped his mouth.

The ring.

She'd forgotten all about the gem she'd stuffed in her pocket, the ring that Sue said had been a present from her husband on their first anniversary.

"I still have a dollar or two."

They talked for a while but Faith's good mood had vanished along with her appetite. Finally, she tossed the rest of her malt into the metal barrel trash can and stood. "You know, it's getting late. We better go home."

"Big plans for tomorrow?"

Faith shrugged, "Not really. I may finally read

one of those romance novels Dora keeps pushing at me.''

Dan laughed and helped her down from her perch on the top of the picnic table. "She loves them. Says the happy ending gets her every time.''

"Must be that matchmaker in her.''

"I'm glad she's outgrown that nonsense.''

"You must be kidding. The woman's a prime example of once a matchmaker, always a matchmaker.''

"Okay,'' Dan said, opening the door of the truck for her. "She might still dabble in it.''

"Dabble?'' Faith raised a brow.

"You know, occasionally try to get some of the singles in the congregation together,'' Dan said. "But I've decided as long as it doesn't involve me, I don't care.''

Amazingly, his sentiments mirrored hers exactly.

"Amen,'' Faith said fervently. "Amen to that.''

Chapter Seven

Tami Edwards's mouth closed over the hamburger. She listened with half an ear to the conversation swirling around her. Normally, she would be the one talking, entertaining her friends Lisa and Amy. They loved her stories. Everyone said she had a real knack for making something boring, exciting. But today her heart wasn't in it. Ever since she'd found out that Faith Richards was staying in the same house with Dan Whitman—her Dan—she hadn't felt much like talking.

She knew better than anyone that visitors to Willow Hill always stayed at the parsonage. After all, her dad was head of the church council. When a minister accepted a call, it was part of the deal.

Until recently, it hadn't mattered who'd stayed under Pastor Dan's roof. But at fifteen, Tami had begun to see the young minister in a different light. Not as a pastor, but as the coolest guy in town. Just one look from those sky-blue eyes was enough to make her melt. Her heart beat a little faster just thinking about how his eyes lingered on her when he preached from the pulpit every Sunday. Sure, he was old. But he was cute. And what did age matter when you're in love?

Well, maybe Dan wasn't in love with her. Yet. But he would be. After all, didn't Tommy Perkins say she was the most beautiful girl he'd ever seen? That all the boys were crazy in love with her? 'Course Tommy was just sixteen, but she was sure he was right. She *was* the prettiest girl in Willow Hill. And she certainly was a whole lot prettier than Faith.

Tami snorted. What kind of name was that anyway? And what about that hair all dark and wind-blown? The moment she'd thought about cutting her hair in that same style, conveniently slipped from her memory.

"My dad says that a woman like her shouldn't be allowed to walk the streets of Willow Hill."

"Does he really think Pastor Dan likes her?"

Tami sat up straighter and dropped the rest of the burger to the plate. "What are you two talking about?"

"I'm sure it's nothing," Amy said, shooting the other girl a warning look. "We all know it's you Pastor Dan likes."

"That's not what my dad says." Lisa shook her head and stabbed a French fry with her fork. "He thinks there's something going on between the two of them. If you know what I mean."

Tami and Amy exchanged glances. They thought they knew what their friend meant, or at least had some idea.

Lisa Lundegard on the other hand, was all too familiar with what she was talking about. Her father's drinking binges, hair-trigger temper and womanizing fueled the small town's gossip mill and exposed his daughter on a daily basis to the different side of life than most of her classmates experienced. It seemed every weekend he left the Wild Horse Saloon with a different woman.

"What makes your father think something's going on?"

"Because my dad and Faith went out the night of the ice cream social."

Amy's eyes widened.

Tami's breath caught in her throat. She leaned forward on the chipped Formica tabletop. "Did she go home with your dad?"

Tami would never have even thought to ask anyone else such a personal question. But "Hank" questions fell into a different category, a familiar one. Every week, Lisa shared her "Hank" stories with her friends. Whom he'd brought home, how many beer cans littered their lawn after one of his drunken binges, stuff like that. Hearing all about

Hank and his exploits rivaled sneaking a peek at the tabloids.

"Naw. He said she wasn't his type."

"I think she's ugly," Tami said.

"Me, too," Amy said loyally.

Lisa just shrugged. "She's all right, I guess. My dad says Dan Whitman sure has the hots for her."

Tami's stomach tightened. "Really?"

"Yep. He said the pastor caused a big scene at Rockwell's Café. Almost fought him over her."

"Did they hit each other?"

"No, my dad said she wasn't worth fightin' over." Lisa's voice lowered conspiratorially. "Way too scrawny."

Tami's finger traced the crack that zigzagged its way across the table. "So, what makes your dad think the pastor likes this woman?"

"He said, in all the years he'd known the man, he'd never seen Dan Whitman so bothered about any broad."

"But she must not be interested in him. Or she wouldn't have gone out with your dad," Tami said hopefully, even though any woman would have to be a total fool to prefer Hank Lundegard to Daniel Whitman.

"Maybe she was trying to make Pastor Dan jealous." Lisa shrugged. "Anyway, the pastor must like her some. The two of them are always together."

Tami's jaw tightened and she pushed the rest of

her food away. That woman didn't belong under the same roof with her Dan.

Tonight might be a good night to spend some time at home. She'd bet anything her dad would be interested in hearing one of her stories. Especially one that involved the kind of person they had staying at the parsonage.

"How's the ankle, Pastor?" Frank Edwards leaned back in the floral chair. The metal frames of his glasses matched the silver at his temples. In his mid-forties, Frank sold insurance for a living and dressed like he was always ready to close a business deal. Although most men in town could be found on a Saturday wearing blue jeans and a flannel shirt, Frank's only concession to the weekend was to leave his suit coat in the closet.

Knowing this, Dan had changed out of his jeans and into a pair of khaki pants before he'd headed over to Frank's house. He still wasn't sure why Frank had called and requested he stop by. Frank would only say that he had something important to discuss that couldn't wait until the next board meeting.

"It's good as new," Dan said, relieved that after almost a week, it was finally the truth. He lifted his leg slightly and rotated his foot to illustrate.

"I heard your houseguest got pulled into duty as your chauffeur."

"Where'd you hear that?" Dan added an extra teaspoon of sugar to his coffee without looking up.

"It's a small town, Pastor," Frank said easily. "People talk. Especially when a single young woman and our equally single pastor seem to be inseparable."

Dan forced a laugh, even though at the moment he didn't find this conversation very amusing. "She helped me out by driving me around until my foot healed. I hardly think 'inseparable' is the word."

"I've heard she's rather an attractive woman." Frank peered over the top of his cup.

"I'm surprised you haven't met her."

"Now, where would I have met her?" A hint of censure crept into Frank's tone. "She hasn't set foot in church since she's been here."

Dan cupped his mug with both hands and reclined against the back of the sofa and waited. Knowing Frank, he had a point, and regardless of Dan's answer, he'd get to it soon enough.

"What do *you* think of your leather-clad guest, Pastor?"

Aha, so that was the issue. Dan shrugged. "She's okay."

"Only okay?" Frank leaned forward, his gaze riveted to Dan. "Some of the men in town seem to think she's a lot more than that."

"Like I said, she's okay." Dan leisurely stretched his suddenly tight muscles. "Where's all this coming from, Frank?"

The older man removed his eyeglasses and wiped each lens carefully with a pristine white handkerchief before speaking. "There's been some talk in town. As head of the church council, I felt it my duty to bring it to your attention."

Dan didn't respond for a moment, a tightness constricting his throat. "What kind of talk?"

Frank's gaze met Dan's head-on. "About whether it's such a good idea for you and that woman to be virtually living together."

"Living together!" Dan dropped his mug to the coffee table with a clatter. His voice rose despite his best efforts to control it. "The woman's a guest at the parsonage, not my live-in lover."

A hint of red darkened Frank's neck, and his lips tightened. "I'll thank you to watch that kind of language, Pastor."

"And I'll thank *you* to watch your insinuations," Dan said, his temper flaring at the injustice of the accusation. "I'd like to think you know me better than that."

"Would anyone like more coffee? Or some cookies?" Joan Edwards stood in the doorway, a silver tray holding a coffeepot and a plate of freshly baked chocolate-chip cookies balanced in her hands.

"None for me, thanks," Dan said.

"Joan, I think we're both fine. Could you pull the door shut on your way out?" Frank's comments may have been worded as a question, but the order was clear.

Her gaze shifted between her husband and Dan. An older version of her daughter, Joan had the same vibrant personality of Tami, with the maturity of twenty-five additional years. She shot Dan a sympathetic smile and pulled the door shut.

Frank stood and pinned Dan with his gaze. "I want you to simmer down and listen for a minute. I'm not the enemy. Remember I was the one that lobbied for you to get this position. Many of the other council members had concerns about calling someone so young. On top of it, you were single. Now having this woman—"

"Her name is Faith Richards," Dan said.

"Whatever," Frank said with a dismissive wave. "Having her under your roof has caused some of those same concerns to rise again."

"You may want to remind those who are so concerned, Frank, that we're not alone in the parsonage. Aunt Dora lives there, too," Dan said smoothly, keeping the irritation from his voice and his expression cool.

"Dan, just listen to me for a minute." Frank placed his eyeglasses back on with a slow deliberate motion. Behind the sparkling clear lenses his gaze was firm and direct, but not unkind. "I'm talking to you now as a friend. And as your friend, I'm warning you. You need to pay attention and avoid even the appearance of impropriety."

"You want me to kick her out?" Dan asked quietly, his fingers tightening around the mug. It wouldn't matter what Frank said, he wasn't about to show Faith the front door. He'd dedicated his life to Christ and he would do the Christian thing regardless of what anyone said or thought.

"No." Frank blew a harsh breath. "I'm not saying that. Just be careful. You're a good minister, Dan. I'd hate for you to have any trouble."

"I appreciate your concern." Dan rose and reached for his coat. "But there's no need for you or anyone else to worry. Ms. Richards and I have very little in common and she's as anxious to blow this town as you are to have her go. I guarantee the minute her Harley is fixed, she'll be out of here."

"Good." The lines around Frank's mouth eased. "Glad to hear it."

Frank walked Dan to the door, his hand resting companionably on the minister's shoulder. "I want you to know I never believed those rumors. I told the others there's no way you could be attracted to a woman who wears black leather and rides a Harley."

Frank's laugh set Dan's teeth on edge.

Dan smiled faintly and reminded himself Frank had only spoken the truth. A small-town minister and a biker from the big city would hardly be a match made in heaven. Still, why did he have the sinking feeling he'd betrayed Faith by not defending her more vigorously?

He shrugged his unease aside. Faith Richards would soon only be a memory. And he'd be once again free to devote his full attention to his ministry.

Chapter Eight

Faith laid the copy of the e-mail on the kitchen table. Dan had volunteered the use of his computer and printer when she'd first arrived and she'd finally taken him up on his offer. She'd spent the morning reading and answering the messages that had accumulated since she'd been on the road. This one totally took her by surprise and she'd had to print it.

She lifted the paper again and reread the words, trying to make sense out of something that made absolutely none.

"Bad news?"

She glanced up. Aunt Dora stood in the doorway, concern evident in her gaze.

"My friend is getting married."

"How wonderful."

"Maybe," Faith said, folding the page precisely in half. "I'm not sure."

Dora hesitated and her expression grew thoughtful. "Is it who she's marrying or just the fact that she's getting married that troubles you?"

Faith sighed and once again glanced down at the sheet. "I guess it's who she's marrying."

What could her friend have been thinking? Marrying such a man? Even Faith, who'd never met him, could tell the minute she'd read the e-mail that he was all wrong. Off the top of her head, she could name dozens of men who'd be a better match for her irrepressible, attractive friend.

Faith cut into the coffee cake she'd made after Dan had left for the office and absently took a piece, mulling over the strange twists in life.

Dora's gaze followed Faith's movements and Faith colored. "I'm sorry, Dora. Would you like a piece?"

Faith held up her cake but Dora waved it aside and sat down at the table. "You say the problem is who she's marrying?"

Faith sighed. Actually it was more what, rather than whom. "He's—"

"Don't tell me." Dora interrupted, raising a bony hand, her eyes sparkling with the love of a good mystery. "Let me guess."

Dora's gaze grew thoughtful, but Faith wasn't fooled. The teasing glint in the woman's pale blue eyes gave her away. "The man's a criminal, struggling to stay one step ahead of the authorities."

Faith lips twitched. She pretended to consider Dora's comments before she shook her head. "No, I'm sure his worst offense is probably no more than a simple parking violation."

"Then he's a wastrel, a man who's never done a day's work in his life."

Faith smiled, hoping when she was eighty-five she would still have such a vivid imagination. "No, he has a steady job."

"Then he's a scoundrel." Dora leaned across the table and fixed her gaze on Faith, her voice lowering to a dramatic whisper. "A playboy with a string of shattered hearts and broken promises a mile wide."

"No, he definitely doesn't sound like the playboy type." Faith chuckled at the look of disappointment that flashed across the older woman's face.

"If the man's not a criminal, a wastrel or a scoundrel, I'm afraid I don't understand," Dora said. "What's the problem?"

Just like Dora had done, Faith leaned over the table and dropped her voice to a whisper. "He's a minister."

"A minister." Dora pretended to shudder. "How horrible."

Faith smiled at the woman's antics, but inwardly she had to sigh. She'd been foolish to think Dora, the consummate matchmaker and a Christian to boot, would understand. "Forget I said anything. It doesn't matter, anyway."

Dora's expression sobered, and it was all Faith could do not to flinch beneath the woman's searching gaze. Sometimes those old eyes saw more than Faith wanted her to see. Like now.

"Oh, my dear, of course it matters." Dora patted her hand, a hint of apology in her tone. "She's your friend and you want her to be happy."

Faith took a bite of the coffee cake, the cinnamon streusel feeling like sand against her tongue. "It's just that I don't think she realizes what she's getting into when she marries a minister."

"Such as?"

"Oh, you know—" The memories of her growing-up years flashed like snapshots in Faith's head: the never-ending church activities, the constant scrutiny, members of the congregation in and out of their home at all hours of the day and night "—like understanding that a minister's job isn't just eight to five. It's a twenty-four-seven commitment."

"Twenty-four-seven?"

Faith smiled. "You know…more than just a full-time job."

Aunt Dora's expression stilled and her gaze searched Faith's face. "Not much of a life. Is that what you're saying?"

"Oh, no," Faith said automatically. "That's not it at all. It can be wonderful for the right person."

Not too many years ago, Faith would have certainly considered working side by side with a minister husband and furthering the Word of the Lord to be an ideal life. Her heart clenched, remembering how much it hurt when she let go of those dreams.

"But not for your friend."

"No. It's not the life for her." *Or for me, either.* "I just can't see her being happy as a minister's wife."

"Perhaps she's changed," Dora suggested gently. "People do, you know."

Faith briefly considered the possibility then quickly discarded it. "It would mean a hundred-and-eighty-degree turnaround."

"Love can do that to a person."

Faith shook her head "I don't buy that."

"You don't believe in the power of love?"

Faith pressed the crumbs against her plate with her fork. "There's not much anymore I do believe in."

"I'm sorry," Dora said softly.

"I'm not," Faith said, raising her gaze to meet Dora's sympathetic one. "I'd rather know the score than waste my life believing in a lie."

"Is that what you think your friend will be doing?" Dora took a sliver of coffee cake from the pan. "Wasting her life?"

Faith got up and turned on the heat under the teakettle. "My friend's career has always meant everything to her."

"There's no reason she can't have her career and marriage, too," Dora pointed out, the modern sentiment surprising Faith. "In fact, most of the candidates our church council interviewed had wives with careers."

"But she's on the road more than she's home," Faith said stubbornly. "There's only so many hours in a day."

"So you're saying she shouldn't work outside of the home?"

"I know this is going to sound strange." Faith fiddled with the knob on the stove, adjusting the height of the flame before raising her gaze. "I think being a minister's wife is a full-time job."

Dora's eyes gleamed and Faith shifted uncomfortably.

How in the world had the subject shifted to her feelings? She wasn't the one marrying the minister. She wouldn't marry a minister if he was the last man on earth, no matter how attractive he was, no matter how charming.

"Really?" A hint of satisfaction crossed Dora's face and she smiled, holding out her cup for some tea.

Faith filled Dora's cup then her own with the steaming water and a tea bag. "I realize it sounds sort of old-fashioned."

"Not old-fashioned," Dora said. "Just realistic."

Dora took a long sip of the orange pekoe blend

and peered at Faith over the top of her cup. "Sounds to me like *you'd* be the perfect minister's wife."

Faith choked, the tea burning her throat. "That's the most ridic— I'm sorry Dora, but just the thought—"

"Tell me, why is it so ridiculous? You're a generous, loving woman who has a lot to offer the right man and the right congregation."

It was ludicrous. Laughable. But for some reason Faith didn't feel like smiling, much less laughing.

"I hate to burst your bubble, but you're forgetting one very important fact. I'm not a believer."

"Oh, my dear." Dora smiled and raised her cup in a mock salute. "There's very little I forget. And even at eighty-five, with my sight failing, very little I can't see."

Faith shook her head and bit back a sharp retort. The matchmaker in Dora had once again overridden the woman's good sense. If Dora truly believed Faith would be the perfect minister's wife, her eyesight was not merely failing, she was obviously blind.

Faith shut the back door and headed across the damp grass toward the gazebo. All her efforts concentrated on not spilling the glass of lemonade in her hand.

If she wouldn't have been such a pig and grabbed four oversized chocolate-chip cookies to take with

her, the task would have been a cakewalk. But now
with the romance novel Aunt Dora had insisted she
take tucked under her arm, one hand holding a tall
tumbler and the other stretched around the cookies,
making it safely to the wooden structure seemed
with every step to be more of an impossibility.

She kept her gaze downward and scanned the
ground ahead like a minesweeper searching for any
treacherous obstacles.

Faith reached the gazebo door and breathed a
sigh of relief. Instead of rushing in and setting her
load on the table before she dropped it, like any
sensible person would have done, she lifted her face
to the sun and let the rays warm her skin. Winter
was fast approaching and Faith knew there
wouldn't be many more days as nice as this one.

Sitting all morning at the computer had been a
necessary evil. With those e-mails read and answered she could now relax and spend the afternoon in the shade, reading her book and gorging
herself on Aunt Dora's homemade cookies. She
stepped inside and immediately stopped short.
"What are *you* doing here?"

"Hello, Faith." Dan laid his pencil down and
lifted his gaze. His lips twitched. "I'm glad to see
you, too."

"I thought you'd gone to the church."

"Obviously not."

She set the glass on the white lacquered table,
dropped the napkin-wrapped cookies beside it and

laid the book facedown. She knew her greeting had been far from gracious but she couldn't hide her disappointment. Her heart fell further at the sight of the open Bible in front of him. "I thought you'd be gone all day."

Dan leaned back on the bench and shrugged. "Sorry to disappoint you."

Faith glanced at the pages of notes scattered across the tabletop and her hopes rose. "Are you almost done?"

"Afraid not." Dan shook his head and his brow furrowed. "I'm having trouble with this sermon and I'm not leaving until I've got it done."

"Sermon?" Faith said weakly.

Dan chuckled. "You know those little talks I give in church every Sunday?"

"I don't go to church, remember?"

"That's right." Dan picked up his pencil and rolled it between his thumb and index finger, his gaze thoughtful as he studied her face.

Faith shifted her gaze back to the house. Dora had shooed her out, saying she was going to be spraying for bugs and the fumes would be horrendous. Personally, Faith thought it was a wasted effort. During her stay at the parsonage she hadn't seen even one tiny little spider.

"Tell me again why you don't go to church?"

Dan's expression was carefully blank but Faith wasn't fooled. He knew very well why she didn't attend services. "Because I don't believe in God. And I won't be a hypocrite."

"That's too bad." Dan shook his head and feigned disappointment. "If you *were* a Christian, you might be able to help me with my sermon."

"Why would I do that?"

"Because," he said, "then I'd get out of here and you'd have the whole place to yourself."

Faith thought for a moment. "Is this some kind of trick?"

"Trick?" Dan raised one brow. "I don't know what you mean."

She hesitated, knowing she was crazy to even consider it. Still, if she helped him finish that— ugh—sermon he would leave and she might be able to salvage the rest of the afternoon. "All right. I'll help you."

"You will?" The look of surprise on his face told her he'd never expected her to agree.

"Of course." Faith picked up a cookie, suddenly pleased with her decision. She took a bite. "You've been so kind to me, how could I not want to help?"

"What about the Christian thing?"

"Speech writers don't have to believe everything they've written." She smiled confidently. Fifteen minutes and he'd be gone. "It'll be easy. You'll see...."

After an hour, Faith was ready to throw in the towel. She wiped a weary hand across her forehead, wondering if politicians were this difficult to please.

Every idea she brought up, he didn't like. Every thought he tried to expound on went nowhere.

Desperate, she handed him one of her precious cookies.

"What's this for?" He held it up as if he'd never seen a double chocolate-chip with walnuts before.

"Energy," Faith said. "Brain power."

He took a bite. Then another. "These are good. Did you bake them?"

"Get real. If I'd made them you wouldn't be able to eat them." She laughed. Once, she'd believed if you could read a recipe it meant you could cook, but she'd soon found out differently. No matter how much she weighed and measured, her outcomes never matched Aunt Dora's thrown-together ones.

"Here." She shoved her half-empty glass of lemonade at him. "Have some of this, too."

He stared at the tumbler. "But this is yours."

"I know it's mine." She heaved an exasperated sigh. "It's also loaded with sugar."

"Brain power?"

"Exactly."

He still hesitated and Faith shook her head. "Don't worry. I don't have any germs. Besides—" she smiled "—you've kissed me before and that didn't seem to bother you any. Drinking after someone isn't a lot different than locking lips with them."

The instant the words left her mouth and his gaze lowered to her lips dusted with cookie crumbs,

Faith knew she was wrong. Kissing *was* different. Feeling the warmth, the sensation of... She shook her head, deliberately breaking the insane spell she'd inadvertently woven. "I've got an idea."

He swallowed a big gulp of her lemonade and brought to his mouth one of the napkins she'd carried with her from the parsonage. "Okay. Lay it on me."

Her gaze followed the napkin and languid warmth filled her limbs. Her heart raced.

"What's your idea?"

Her head jerked up and he smiled as if he knew what she'd been thinking hadn't had one thing to do with the sermon.

"Plato's Allegory of the Cave." The words popped out, surprising even her.

His eyelashes flickered.

"Are you familiar with it?"

"I hadn't thought about it in years." A thoughtful expression crossed Dan's face. "It might work."

Unable to sit still, Faith rose and stood behind Dan. She leaned over and rested one hand lightly on his shoulder, scanning the outline in front of him.

"It would dovetail nicely here." She pointed to a section they'd worked on earlier. "Right where you start talking about the change that occurs in your life when you truly see the Light."

Dan tapped his fingers on the table and stared at the page.

She held her breath. "What do you think?"

"I think you've got it."

Excitement surged in Faith. For years she'd helped her father with his sermons, and she'd forgotten how invigorating it could be.

"*We* got it," she said with a saucy smile. "This was a joint effort."

"You're right," he said softly, answering her smile with a grin of his own. "And to God be the glory."

Dora pushed aside the lace curtain of the second-floor bedroom with a bony finger, barely listening to her sister's voice chattering on the other end of the line. She was tempted to tell Edith she'd have to call her back. After all, she had more important things to attend to than listen to Edith tell her how often her neighbor let out his dog.

The spraying-for-bugs idea had worked like magic. When she'd encouraged Faith to spend the afternoon reading in the gazebo, Dora saw no need to mention that Dan was already out there working on his sermon for Sunday.

She pressed her nose close to the windowpane. It was impossible to see directly into the gazebo from any angle except this one, but the distance presented another problem. Where were those bird-watching binoculars of hers anyway?

She settled for squinting. The sight of Faith's dark head bent over Dan's blond one sent her tired blood surging like an awakened river. Dora leaned even closer and squinted. Was that Faith's hand resting on Dan's shoulder? Was he smiling up at her?

So far, so good. It was working out just as she'd hoped but she needed to keep things rolling. It was time to kick her plan into high gear.

"Edith." Dora interrupted her sister without a second thought. "I've decided to change my plans. Instead of next week, I'll be stopping by tomorrow."

"Will Dan be bringing you?" Edith loved to visit with the young minister.

"Not this time," Dora said. "Ray will bring me."

She made a mental note to call her nephew and let him know he'd be making the trip with her. Saturday was a busy day at the garage, but Ray could work late tonight to make up for being gone tomorrow. With his wife and children out of town, there was no reason he had to be home early.

Dora finalized her plans with Edith, then glanced out the window one last time.

Her heart warmed. Her new plan was a stroke of genius. She needed Dan to realize Faith would be the perfect minister's wife and for Faith to realize that God still lived in her heart.

A difficult task to be sure, but wasn't she a master matchmaker with over sixty years of experience in the field? All credit, of course, going to her life-long partner. Dora lifted her gaze and said a word-less thank-you.

Satisfied with what she'd accomplished in the last few hours, Dora let the curtain fall back and headed for the refrigerator. She and Ray would be leaving at the crack of dawn so she'd better get cooking. Faith would have enough to do without worrying about the food.

She smiled. Faith would fit in perfectly with Dan and his friends. Tomorrow night he'd see that for himself, and Dora would be one step closer to mak-ing a spring wedding a reality.

Chapter Nine

Faith hurried down the hall, eager to savor a cup of Aunt Dora's industrial-strength coffee. Since she'd been in Willow Hill, Faith had found herself taking after the natives, going to bed early and rising when the sun had barely had a chance to settle itself in the sky. The trouble was, although the body may be willing, her brain hadn't quite got the message. It was still operating in a sleep-deprived fog.

She cast a glance at the clock on the wall and cringed. No wonder she craved the caffeine. It was barely past seven! If she continued getting up earlier every day—as she had this past week—it wouldn't be long before she'd be rolling out of bed at the crack of dawn.

She shuddered at the thought and pushed against the kitchen door. It swung open easily, but Faith paused at the threshold, puzzled. Every Saturday, Aunt Dora had buttermilk pancakes and bacon waiting, the coffee perking and the table set for breakfast.

Faith's gaze slid around the empty room. Where *was* Aunt Dora? And, more important, where was that coffee?

A canary-yellow scrap of paper caught her eye. Faith snatched it off the table and read it quickly. The message was clear. Her caffeine-starved brain and growling stomach would have to wait a few more minutes.

Faith sighed. She'd looked forward all week to those pancakes, but now she was forced to fend for herself. Resigned to her fate, she started the coffee and dropped a couple of slices of Dora's homemade raisin bread into the toaster.

While the coffee brewed, Faith picked up the paper Dora had left neatly folded on the counter. Willow Hill's paper only came out weekly, so Dan subscribed to the one out of Norfolk, the nearest "big" town.

Faith had discovered she enjoyed reading the news from the region even though she wasn't sure where most of the towns mentioned in the stories were located and she didn't know any of the people quoted.

"Dora." The door to the kitchen swung open. "About tonight..."

"She's not here." Faith lowered the paper and glanced up.

Like she herself had done only moments before, Dan's gaze quickly scanned the room. "Where is she?"

Faith shrugged and gestured to the piece of paper. "She left a note."

Dan glanced briefly in that direction but made no move to pick it up. His gaze instead riveted to her stocking feet propped on his chair.

"What?"

Dan directed another pointed glance at her red socks. Faith shifted her feet to the floor and he took the spot they'd just vacated.

He'd barely gotten settled when the coffeemaker beeped—an irritating but welcome sound. Dan jumped up. "I'll get it."

She smiled. Apparently she wasn't the only one who liked coffee first thing in the morning.

He headed straight for the cupboard. With well-practiced ease he retrieved two tall ceramic cups from the upper shelf and filled them to the brim with the steaming brew. He set one of the mugs down in front of her and kept the other cupped in his hand.

Dan slid back into the seat across from Faith and reached for the note. Faith sipped the hot hazelnut blend and peered over the top of her cup, unobtrusively studying him. Even at seven in the morning the guy looked fabulous. His just-washed hair gleamed in the fluorescent light and the slate-colored plaid shirt brought out the blue in his eyes. Faith could hardly believe this handsome hunk was a minister. Her father had never looked that good in a button-down shirt.

Dan studied the note. She studied him.

His eyes darkened and his jaw tightened. He crumpled the message into a tiny ball.

"What's wrong?"

Dan sighed. "Dora went to see her sister. Sounds like some sort of family emergency. Ray picked her up early this morning and they headed to Norfolk. That's where Edith lives."

Faith knew just where Dora's sister lived—in a tall white house with a wraparound porch and hollyhocks lining the walk. She and Dora had gone shopping one day and had impulsively stopped at her sister's, hoping to catch her at home. But only a tiger-striped cat sitting on the rail had been there to greet them. Edith, whom Dora affectionately referred to as a gadabout, was nowhere to be found.

"I hope she's okay. Dora and her sister are pretty close." When she was little, Faith had prayed for a sister. Now, looking back, she could see it was only the beginning of a long string of unanswered prayers.

"We'll pray for her," Dan said.

You'll pray for her.

The toaster popped up and Faith headed for the

toaster, reveling in the aroma of freshly warmed bread.

"Any idea how long she'll be gone?" Faith said over her shoulder, slathering the hot bread with the sweet cream butter. She'd read the note so fast she couldn't really remember what it said.

Dan leaned back in his chair. He shook his head and a worried frown furrowed his brow. "I'm guessing at least tonight. Maybe most of the weekend."

He waved away a slice of toast impatiently. Dora's note had clearly upset Dan. But why? Granted, Dora made most of the meals, but tonight that wouldn't be a problem because of the barbecue.

The barbecue.

Suddenly she understood. She raised her gaze to find Dan staring. A chill coursed through her at the hopeful light in his eyes.

She dropped the half-eaten piece of bread to the plate and shifted her gaze away. Perhaps she still had time to make her escape. Faith rose and kept her eyes fixed firmly on the door. "I just remembered somewhere I need to be."

It was a lame excuse but she'd never been at her best under pressure.

"Faith." Dan's hand brushed her arm, and the heat from his touch threatened to short-circuit her good sense.

"I need to talk to you."

She reluctantly stopped and turned. "I don't have much time."

"This won't take long." He flashed her a smile and pushed up from the chair, standing so close to her, she wondered if he could see her heart beating through the thin cotton of her shirt. "I promise."

What was there about a man saying those two little words? She raised her gaze, looked into those baby blues and turned spineless as a jellyfish. "Okay. One minute. That's all."

"Couldn't I please have two?" A dimple in his cheek flashed.

Faith narrowed her gaze even as her heart picked up speed. This guy had charm down to an exact science. She gave in to the inevitable and plopped down.

"I don't know why I'm so nervous."

Strangely, Dan's little laugh coupled with his words touched her more than a bold confidence ever could. Faith couldn't help it. She gave him an encouraging smile.

He returned it and took a deep breath. "Aunt Dora was supposed to act as the hostess for the barbecue tonight and I thought…well, I hoped…you could help me out and fill in?"

Dan's words came out in a rush and she could tell he was desperate. Faith hesitated, forcing herself to remember what he was asking of her and why she had to say no.

"Dan." She took a deep breath and clenched her

hands in her lap. "If it was a community event, maybe. But I can't act as your hostess for a bunch of ministers and their wives. I would rath—"

Faith stopped herself just in time. Even though she *would* rather face a pack of rabid dogs, she didn't think Dan would appreciate the comparison. "I just can't."

She shoved her chair back with a clatter.

"Faith, please. I'm in a real bind here or I wouldn't ask." His words ran together and she could hear the panic behind them. "I need you."

"You don't need *me*." She lifted her chin and hardened her heart against his boyish appeal. "You just need *someone*. I happen to know there are lots of women in your church who would be thrilled to be asked."

"I don't want them."

Her heart skipped a beat. "Why not?"

"Because they might misunderstand and think that I…" His voice trailed off and a slight flush reddened his neck.

"So that's it." Faith's voice was flat and she fought to keep the emotions surging through her body off her face. "You're worried they might misunderstand and think that you liked them. While I, on the other hand, would have no such illusions."

"Faith, you know I like…"

She silenced him with a glance. "Am I right? Yes or no?"

"You're right," he said finally. "But that's not the only consideration."

She raised a brow.

"Dora's the real reason I want you to do this. I'm sure she feels really bad about leaving me in the lurch," he said. "If you filled in for her, well, that would be one thing. But if someone else did, she'd feel even worse, thinking she really let me down. Next time something like this comes up, I'm afraid she might not go."

The sincerity in his face was evident. Faith shifted uncomfortably. Dora had been so good to both of them. Dan couldn't let her down. Could she?

"I suppose I could make the big sacrifice and spend the evening with a bunch of old ladies." Just the thought made her half-sick.

"I know this isn't easy for you...."

"You're right about that," she said promptly, forestalling any more discussion. "I'll be missing all my favorite television shows."

Dan smiled and squeezed her hand. To his credit he chose not to point out the obvious: Faith never watched TV.

"Your mother looked splendid." Dora sipped her tea and took another bite of the gingersnap. "I was glad we were able to see her before she left on her trip."

Ray opened his refrigerator and grabbed a beer.

"She's only going to Kansas City for a few days, for goodness—" Dora's cane whacked his leg and Ray stopped short, feeling all of ten years old. He bit back a sharp retort and resisted the urge to rub his aching shin. "I'm just saying I don't know what was so all-fired important that I had to take off work and drive all the way to Norfolk."

"Edith wanted to ask me about some of our relatives she's planning to see," Dora said in that slow patient voice that always made him feel stupid. "I remember them better than she does. We quit spending summers down there when your mother was just a little girl."

"What was wrong with just calling her on the phone?"

Dora shot him a reproving look. "You know your mother doesn't hear that well anymore."

"She hears just fine when she wants to," Ray muttered, remembering the times he'd mistakenly thought his mother had been too far away to hear his under-the-breath comments.

"Raymond." Dora's voice held a hint of warning and he almost smiled. She'd never allowed him to criticize his mother when he'd been a child. Why had he ever thought she'd let him start now?

"It was a beautiful day for a drive and it had been far too long since we'd seen her."

"I still don't see why it had to be today." Ray downed the last of his beer and wiped his mouth with the back of his hand. "We're real busy down at the shop. Say—'' he narrowed his gaze ''—speakin' of the shop, when can I get that Harley out of there? It's taking up valuable space.''

"The time's not right." Dora took another one of the cookies Ray had dumped on an old melamine plate. "For now, when Faith calls, just keep doing what you've been doing."

Ray leaned back and loosened the top button of his pants. "You want me to keep lying?"

"Raymond, what am I going to do with you?" Dora heaved an exasperated sigh. "Once her motorbike is finished, Faith will leave Willow Hill. And I absolutely will not allow that to happen."

Ray made a show of glancing at the clock. He'd learned long ago not to argue with his aunt. "Look how late it's getting. I'd better get you home."

"No need. I've decided to stay the night." Dora tapped her cane and glanced around the kitchen. Her eyes shifted to the stack of unwashed dishes lining the counters, and Ray's misgivings increased by each second her gaze lingered. "With Helen and the children visiting her mother, you need some help."

"I'm doing great."

Her gaze returned to the counter. She raised a brow and said nothing.

Ray stirred uneasily in the chair, and under Dora's steady scrutiny he struggled to think of an excuse why she shouldn't stay. "Isn't this the weekend for that big shindig at the parsonage?"

Something flickered far back in Dora's pale eyes. "Shindig?"

Sometimes she chattered so much, he just tuned her out. Ray fought to remember what she'd told him. "Yeah, you know, that picnic thing for those ministers? They come every year and you take care of the wives."

"Oh, that," Dora said, her face expressionless.

"Isn't that tonight?" Ray couldn't keep the hopeful eagerness from his voice.

"Indeed, you're quite right."

"Pastor Dan will be expecting you." Ray smiled with newfound hope. In a few minutes he'd be home free. He tried not to be overconfident. "C'mon, let's go."

"I'm not going anywhere," Dora announced, taking another sip of her tea. "As I said before, I'm staying. You and I are going to spend a nice quiet evening together."

Ray stifled a groan and cast another look at the clock hanging askew on the wall. Jack and the guys would be here in less than an hour. They'd had this poker game planned for over a month.

He gave it another try, not caring if he sounded desperate. "But who's going to take care of the ladies? The pastor needs you."

Dora couldn't keep a satisfied smile from her lips. Ray didn't fool her in the least. He wasn't concerned about Dan's predicament. Rather, she suspected, he was trying to dump her. With his wife and children out of town, it would be a perfect time for Ray and his friends to smoke cigars, drink beer and play that awful poker game.

"He's got Faith there. She'll help him out." Dora contentedly took another sip of tea and her old body vibrated with new life. Staying with her nephew tonight had been a stroke of genius, if she did say so herself. This plan would serve not one, but two purposes. It would keep Ray on the straight and narrow and give Dan another opportunity to see just what a wonderful minister's wife Faith would make.

Her smile widened at the thought of a May wedding. Perhaps if it was set late enough they could even use fresh flowers from the garden. The whole plan had an indefinable feeling of rightness.

"Ray, if you would be so kind as to refill my hot water, we can get started."

"Get started?" Ray leaned forward, his elbows on the table, his eyes wary.

"Why, stuffing those Sunday school packets I brought over, of course."

Dora ignored Ray's groan and heaved a contented sigh. Life didn't get much better than this.

Chapter Ten

The front door chimed and Faith rushed from her bedroom. She stood for a long moment at the top of the stairs and wondered once again why she'd ever said yes.

The question had tortured her all afternoon, and she still hadn't come up with an answer that made any sense. She had concluded that Dan's concern over Aunt Dora's feelings had been a ruse, his way of solving a last-minute problem with the least amount of effort. No phone calls, no arrangements, no hassle.

Although she'd concede having her stand in for Dora made sense from a purely convenience standpoint, the plan had a fatal flaw. A non-Christian playing hostess to a gathering of rural ministers and their wives was clearly crazy. Her agreeing to do it was just as nuts.

Her feet itched to slip out the back door. There were plenty of other things to do tonight, such as walk around the lake or catch a movie at the theater downtown. Even balancing her checkbook sounded appealing. But Faith knew she was kidding no one, least of all herself. She wouldn't pursue any of these options. She couldn't. She'd given her word.

Voices from the foyer floated up the stairs, and Faith straightened, like a condemned prisoner bravely ready to face a firing squad. She ran a hand through her slightly damp hair and cast one final glance at the outfit she'd pieced together only moments before.

She'd coupled a long stretchy black skirt with a grape-colored V-necked shell and matching cardigan. The soft cashmere clung to her curves and the flowing lines accentuated her willowy figure.

Faith stared thoughtfully at the makeshift outfit and, for an instant, a hint of uncertainty slipped through her confident façade. She knew the outfit looked good on her, but would it be too trendy for tonight's gathering? Maybe a touch too flattering? Faith immediately shoved aside the concerns. This skirt and sweater was the best her limited wardrobe had to offer, and it would simply have to do.

She squared her shoulders and reminded herself that the sooner she got going, the sooner it would be over. With a sigh of resignation, Faith pasted a smile on her face and slipped down the stairs.

"Faith, I wondered where you were." Dan

looked up and smiled, and if he was disappointed in what she'd worn, it didn't show. "I'd like you to meet Reverend Stephens and his wife."

"Call me Ron." The balding, pleasant-faced man extended his hand. "This is my wife, Marjorie."

"Faith Richards," she said, shaking their hands. "Pleased to meet you."

The minister's curious gaze moved from Dan to Faith, before exchanging a look with his wife.

"Faith is a houseguest here at the parsonage." Dan placed his hand on her shoulder. "She's pinch-hitting for Aunt Dora this evening."

"Is Dora ill?" Marjorie's brow furrowed in concern.

"She's fine," Dan quickly assured her. "But her sister is a bit under the weather. Dora wanted to spend some time with her, so Faith is pinch-hitting."

Faith hid a smile. Though no one else would probably notice, she could tell Dan was not his normal confident self.

In a matter of minutes the other five couples arrived and Faith decided if she heard the term "pinch-hitting" one more time, she'd upchuck all over Dora's just-polished wood floors.

With the introductions out of the way, Dan appeared to relax and Faith's earlier worries slipped away. The group was friendly, and networking appeared to be the primary focus. As pastors of rural congregations, these ministers were more isolated from their peers, and occasions like these allowed them to get together on a purely social basis with others who shared their day-to-day challenges.

After about two hours, Faith concluded she and Dan made a dynamite team. In between refilling platters with the mountains of food Aunt Dora had prepared, they'd mingled and made sure all of the guests had a good time.

Dan knew everyone, but for Faith the task of keeping names and faces straight proved daunting. Not only had she never been good with names but, to compound the problem, the men looked like they'd all popped out of the same mold: early to mid-thirties, clean-cut, slightly receding hair line with about fifteen pounds of extra baggage around their midsection.

Dan Whitman was the one exception, the man who'd broken the mold. Her gaze searched the room and located him by the fireplace. He stood with one hand resting on the mantel, the other holding a glass of sparkling apple cider. A good five years younger than his peers, he wore the same casual uniform, dress pants and a long-sleeve cotton shirt, but there was no mistaking his muscular build and no doubt this was one man without an extra ounce of fat. His thick golden hair was lush and full. Quite simply he was gorgeous.

Faith sighed.

"He's very handsome, isn't he?"

Faith's gaze jerked from Dan to find Marjorie Stephens staring at her with a knowing smile.

"Dan? I mean Pastor Whitman?" She stumbled over the words like a nervous schoolgirl.

"Who else?" Marjorie picked up a carrot stick from the relish tray on the coffee table. "You two make such a cute couple."

Cute couple? She and Dan?

Faith's lips quirked. She toyed with the notion of using Dan's line and telling Marjorie she was just "pinch- hitting," but the words lodged in her throat and she remained silent.

"I really like your outfit." Marjorie touched the skirt of her own rayon suit. "Dora always has dressed more formally and we've always followed her lead, but I'm ready for a change. How about next year we make it even more casual—maybe khakis or jeans?"

"Great idea, but I won't be here then." Faith grabbed a piece of celery and took a bite, wondering how the woman could have gotten the impression she was staying. Dan's repeated comments about "pinch-hitting" must have sailed right over her head.

"But why not?" Marjorie snapped the carrot stick in two. "I've been watching you and Dan all evening. His eyes follow you everywhere."

Faith refrained from telling the woman that Dan was probably watching to make sure she didn't pull some major social faux pas.

"You like him, too, don't you?" Marjorie said in a low conspiratorial tone.

Faith choked on her celery and Marjorie smiled with satisfaction.

"Marjorie," Faith said once she caught her breath, "you've got it all wrong."

"Who's got what wrong?" Dan's voice sounded behind her, and the musky scent of his cologne sent her heart racing.

Her companion's eyes gleamed behind her wire-framed glasses and, if Marjorie wasn't fifty years too young, for a second Faith would have sworn it was Aunt Dora beside her with a Cheshire cat grin on her face. "I was just telling Faith what a cute couple you two make. She denied it, of course, but I think…" Marjorie cocked her head as if listening to some far-off sound. "Yes, I'm definitely hearing wedding bells."

Dan blanched.

Faith couldn't help but chuckle.

He shot her a quelling glance. "Marjorie, I know you fancy yourself somewhat of a matchmaker, but this time you're way off the mark."

Faith's gaze shot to Marjorie, and not only didn't the woman seem offended by Dan's words, she actually seemed pleased. Marjorie Stephens *was* definitely another Aunt Dora. A little younger, a little plumper, but just as determined. It was too bad Dan couldn't lighten up and see the humor of the situation even if she couldn't see it herself a minute ago.

"A spring wedding would be nice," Marjorie said as if he'd never spoken.

Dan's eyes flashed and he held up a hand. "Faith and I are friends, Marjorie. Just friends, nothing more. In fact, she'll be leaving Willow Hill in the dust as soon as her motorcycle is repaired."

Marjorie sat up straight, her brown eyes flashing with unrestrained interest. "What kind of motorcycle?"

"A Harley," Faith answered.

"You own a Harley-Davidson?" Admiration sounded in the woman's voice. "Ron and I have talked for years about getting one."

"Really?" Faith couldn't imagine Marjorie and the mild-mannered Ron on a Hog.

"Our dream is to go to Sturgis for the big rally." The woman's face took on a positively dreamy expression.

"Sturgis?" Dan's mouth dropped open. "You've got to be kidding!"

"Yes, Sturgis. And no, I'm not kidding." Marjorie laughed, a pleasant tinkling sound, and Faith found herself liking this woman despite her matchmaking attempts. "Don't sound so shocked, Dan. There are lots of ministers who make the trek to South Dakota every year. They hold church services on Sunday and participate in lots of the activities. Granted, the crowd isn't what you'd call traditional, but since when did the Lord say to minister only to the mainstream?''

Dan stared, dumbfounded, and Marjorie shifted her attention to Faith. "What kind do you have?"

Faith smiled. "A Road King Classic. In lazer red pearl."

Marjorie nodded, clearly impressed. "We're thinking of getting a Fat Boy."

"What color?"

"Sinister blue pearl."

"I love that shade."

"Me, too."

The two giggled and Dan shook his head in stunned disbelief.

Faith thought back to how scared she'd been when she'd first laid eyes on the cycle. Her father had taught her to ride when she was in her teens. Like his brother, he'd been somewhat of a motorcycle junkie. But she'd never been on anything near the size of the Road King Classic. Despite her initial apprehension, she'd enjoyed riding the big Hog. Strange as it sounded, traveling down the open road had given her back herself. She'd been able to think and reflect on all that had happened in the past year.

Unfortunately, just when she'd started feeling good about leaving God behind, that blasted deer had appeared out of nowhere and she'd been propelled back into a world she wanted no part of: a world of ministers and their wives, of Bible studies and church.

"I said, did you have to order it? Or did you buy it off the floor?"

Faith started and realized Marjorie had been waiting for an answer. "Actually, it's my uncle's. He ordered it through a dealership in Kansas City. Uncle George planned to fly down from his home in South Dakota and then drive it back."

"The cycle is your uncle's?" Dan raised a brow and she realized she'd somehow forgotten to mention the cycle wasn't hers.

She nodded.

"I guess I don't understand," Dan said with a puzzled expression. "If it's his, what are you doing with it?"

"I'm the delivery girl," Faith said lightly, shifting her gaze to the sparkling amber of the cider. "Uncle George had unexpected bypass surgery last month."

"Is he going to be okay?" Marjorie covered Faith's hand with hers and her voice radiated concern.

Faith swallowed hard. Her uncle's illness following so close on the heels of her parents' deaths had knocked her for a loop. "The doctors are saying he'll recover completely."

"Praise the Lord," Marjorie said.

Faith stiffened and pressed her lips together.

Dan's gaze shot to Faith.

She shifted her gaze and said nothing. The silence stretched uncomfortably.

"I'll bet seeing his new Harley will cheer him up." Marjorie's curious gaze shifted between Faith and Dan.

"I hope so," Faith said. "He doesn't even know I'm coming. It's supposed to be a surprise."

"Does he know you wrecked it?" Dan asked with concern.

Faith shook her head.

"You wrecked your uncle's motorcycle?" Marjorie said in a hushed shocked voice, her hand rising to her throat. "Oh, my goodness. How horrible. A brand-new Harley. You must feel simply terrible."

The sick feeling that had swept over Faith when she'd seen what she'd done to the beautiful Hog returned with a vengeance.

"It was an accident. A deer jumped out in front of her." Dan gave Faith's shoulder a comforting squeeze. "It wasn't her fault."

"I'm sorry." Marjorie cast Faith an apologetic glance. "I didn't mean—"

"Don't worry about it." Faith waved her silent. "I'm sure it'll be as good as new once it's fixed."

If it's ever fixed.

Faith jumped up, eager to change the subject. "I think I'll get us all some more cider."

Dan's gaze followed her until she disappeared into the kitchen. He turned to find Marjorie staring.

"I didn't mean to make her feel bad," Marjorie said, her voice cracking.

"You didn't." Dan gave her hand a reassuring squeeze, ashamed of his earlier response. Something in him had snapped when he'd seen the pain on Faith's face. "I'm sorry I was so abrupt."

"I wouldn't have hurt her for the world."

"I know that."

"I like her, Dan."

"She's a good person," he said cautiously, the gleam in Marjorie's brown eyes sending up red flags.

"You two make a great-looking couple. Why, you're practically guaranteed beautiful children."

Dan choked on the last of his cider. "Marge, listen to me. You've got this all wrong. Faith's a houseguest, nothing more."

From across the room Faith's laughter reached his ears; Dan automatically turned toward the sound.

"A houseguest you can't keep your eyes off of," Marjorie pointed out.

"Marge—"

To his irritation, the woman laughed at his warning growl.

"Lighten up, Dan. I'm tired of waiting for you to find a wife. Frankly, I'm fed up with all your excuses." Marjorie's gaze lingered on Faith across the room. "So, I've taken it into my own hands and picked her myself. Faith is perfect."

"Why? Because she rides a Harley and knows what a Fat Boy is?"

"Works for me." Marjorie laughed and her eyes twinkled. "Actually, I was serious about us all going to Sturgis next summer."

Dan heaved an exasperated sigh. How had things gotten so out of control? If this went much further, Marjorie would have her husband in the parlor ready to read the wedding vows. "You can't be serious. You've known Faith for barely two hours and yet you're convinced she's the one for me?"

"Some things a woman just knows."

"You just know," Dan repeated slowly, wondering if Marjorie would feel the same way if she knew Faith wasn't a Christian?

Telling Marjorie would be one way to put a firm stop to the woman's blatant matchmaking, but for some reason Dan couldn't say the words.

"Call it woman's intuition," Marjorie said with a confident air. "I sense the Lord's hand in this. I can see it now." Marjorie spread her hands and held them up as if framing a picture. "Ron and I on one cycle, you and Faith on the other, traveling down the highway for Christ."

Dan shook his head. "You've got some imagination."

"Don't tell me you can't picture it."

He chuckled and ignored her probing glance, not wanting her to know that for the briefest of seconds he could see it.

And it scared him to death.

* * *

"Whew." Dan collapsed onto the couch. "I'm glad that's over."

"Actually—" Faith scraped leftover potato salad and baked beans from a plate into the plastic garbage bag "—it wasn't so bad."

In fact, the evening had wildly surpassed her admittedly low expectations. The couples had all seemed genuinely glad to meet her and had welcomed her into their close-knit group with open arms. Her only regret had been in turning down their repeated offers to get together again.

She'd be leaving soon, she'd told them. But even if she weren't planning to head out on the open road the minute her cycle was fixed, it would never work. Dan Whitman and Faith Richards would never be a couple, no matter how much Marjorie and Aunt Dora plotted.

Faith plopped down next to Dan, suddenly exhausted. "That Marjorie is really something, isn't she?"

"She didn't mean to make you feel bad about the Harley," Dan said quietly.

Faith glanced down at her lap and picked at a stray piece of lint. "I know she didn't."

Dan leaned forward and rested his elbows on his knees. "I'm surprised you never mentioned it was your uncle's bike and not yours."

Faith rubbed the bridge of her nose and tried to remember why she'd never told him.

"Faith." Dan's eyes were dark and probing in the soft lamplight. "Why was it such a big secret?"

"I guess it never came up?"

"Try again."

"I don't know why, Dan." She blew out a weary breath. "Let's just drop it. I'll be gone soon, and I'm beginning to think the less involved we are in each other's lives, the better."

"Less involved?" Dan said in a light tone. "Marjorie's already planning the wedding."

He'd meant the words to be teasing. But the minute they popped out and his gaze met hers, his smile faded.

Faith drew her tongue over her suddenly dry lips. "Yeah, she said pretty much the same thing to me. Crazy, huh?"

Dan leaned back against the couch and slowly turned his head to her. "Yeah, crazy."

Their gazes locked and their breathing came in unison. Faith's palms grew damp. She stood and reached for the garbage sack, the movement breaking the spell. "Why don't you go to bed? I'll finish up."

"You're not cleaning up this mess. I am." Dan took the plastic bag from her hands. "You go to bed. I'm just going to sit here a few minutes and see if I can get rid of this headache."

For the first time, Faith noticed the lines of strain around his eyes. The night had taken its toll.

Without saying a word, she headed into the

kitchen and returned moments later with a glass of
water and two aspirin.

"Take these."

"Are you pushing pills again?" Dan said with a
weak smile. "Or is it just my imagination?"

Faith chuckled, remembering his reluctance to
take anything after his ankle injury. "It's just your
imagination."

"In that case..." Dan took the pills from her
hand, popped them in his mouth and washed them
down with a long drink of the water.

He straightened upright and winced.

Faith's narrowed her gaze. "Your head must really hurt."

Dan closed his eyes and leaned back against the
sofa's soft fabric. "Yeah, it does."

"Let me try something." Faith moved around
the back of the couch. "Unbutton your collar and
loosen your tie."

"Why?"

"Just do it," she said in the nurse voice she'd
had such success with before.

He heaved an exasperated sigh, but his hand
slipped to his neck and he loosened the tight knot
and slipped open the collar button. "Did anyone
ever tell you that you were bossy?"

"All the time," Faith said with a grin. "Now
lean forward just a bit."

He shifted and Faith dipped her hands inside his
shirt.

His head jerked up. "What the—"

"Just relax," Faith said in a calm, soothing voice. "Close your eyes."

Surprisingly he did.

Once again her fingers moved to knead the bunched muscles. She probed deep into the tight knots in his shoulders. Her mother had taught her well. About once a month her father would get all stiff and sore, and Faith loved to rub his neck. Some of her best memories centered on those times and their long talks.

Dan's skin was warm and smooth beneath her touch, and she quickly realized she'd been naive in thinking this would be just like massaging her father's neck. The closeness and intimacy of her contact with Dan caught her off guard.

"Oh, wow." Dan exhaled a long breath. "That feels great."

"Does it?" Her heart skipped a beat.

"Mmm-hmm." Dan kept his eyes closed but a tiny smile tipped his lips.

She remembered those lips and how soft they'd been when they'd kissed her. She remembered the strength of his arms when he'd pulled her close. She remembered how much she'd wanted to kiss him again. As much as she wanted to kiss him now.

His breathing slowed and she could tell he'd fallen into a light sleep. Her fingers barely moved against his skin, but she couldn't bear to break the contact. What was there about this man that made it so difficult for her to keep her distance?

Across the room an antique picture of Jesus in an oval frame stared knowingly at her. She jerked her hands from Dan's neck and stumbled backward.

What in the world had she been thinking?

"What?" Dan stirred and slowly opened his eyes. "What's the matter?"

"Back rub's over," Faith said abruptly. "It's getting late."

She brushed past him and reached for the sack at his feet. He grabbed her hand.

"Hey, wait," he said. "Not so fast. I didn't even get a chance to thank you for tonight."

"I didn't do anything." She tried to pull her hand away but he held on tight.

"Yes, you did. You were the perfect hostess. Everyone loved you."

"Yeah, well, they don't really know me, do they?" She ignored the tightness gripping her chest. "I don't think they'd feel the same way if they knew I didn't share their beliefs."

"They'd still like you," Dan said softly. "And God would still love you. He will never quit loving you, no mat—"

Faith closed his lips with her fingers. "Don't. Not tonight. It's been a perfect evening. Please don't ruin it by preaching."

Her chin lifted and Dan's words about God's grace died in his throat. She was right. It had been a perfect evening and he had no desire to end it with an argument, especially with someone as stubborn and headstrong as Faith Richards.

Arguing would get him nowhere. He'd have to find a different way to break through Faith's hurt-filled shell and guide her back to the Light. If he only knew how to do it.

Idly his gaze wandered around the room, stopping on a familiar picture. Why had he ever thought he was in this battle alone? A sense of peace stole over him and he smiled.

With Him on Dan's side, Faith didn't stand a chance.

Chapter Eleven

❧

"What do you mean it's still back-ordered? It's been over a month already." Faith ran her fingers through her hair. She bit her tongue to still the angry words that threatened to spill. How long had she listened to Ray give her the same lame excuse? When he promised to call his distributor again, she barely stopped herself from saying, "Don't bother."

With the forecast of snow for next week, if she didn't get out of Willow Hill soon, she'd be stuck here forever. When part of her wondered if that wouldn't be all bad, she realized she'd already stayed too long.

Despite her best attempts to keep Dan Whitman at arm's length, he'd gradually insinuated his way into her life. And heart. Every morning they ate breakfast together. Over a cup of coffee and maybe some eggs and toast, they'd discuss a variety of topics: the upcoming day's events, national and local news, even, Faith shuddered, religion.

Grudgingly she admitted he voiced some valid points. If he would have beaten her over the head with his opinion, her walls would have been up and ready. But the more she got to know Dan, the more she'd come to realize that wasn't his style.

He lived his belief, showing by example what it meant to be a Christian. In the deep recesses of her heart she'd found herself wondering if he might just be right. Wondering if maybe, just maybe, she'd been too quick to cast God aside.

Each day she vowed the time had come to break the comfortable routine and end the closeness. But every morning she'd wander down to the kitchen table and her heart would leap at the sight of him sitting there, warming his hands around a cup of coffee.

He'd glance up at her footsteps and his blue eyes would sparkle in welcome. Even with his golden curls all tousled from sleep, and dressed in what he called his "I-just-got-up-clothes"—an old flannel shirt hugging his broad chest, and ragged jeans— he put the GQ models to shame.

Like a robot, Faith followed the aroma of freshly brewed coffee to the kitchen.

Dan lowered his paper, his eyes glancing at the clock. "Good morning, Sleepyhead."

"Sleepyhead!" Faith pretended to bristle. "I'll have you know I was up when the chicken crowed."

A smile quirked the sides of Dan's lips. "Chicken?"

Faith grinned and realized she definitely needed some caffeine. She reached for the coffeepot. "You know what I meant."

"What do you have planned today?" Dan asked, leaning back in his chair. The hint of whisker stubble grazed his cheeks. Obviously he hadn't been up with the chickens, either.

Faith shrugged. "Not much. I just talked to Ray and my parts are still not in."

"Think you might have time to dub some sermon tapes for me today? Harold called and asked if you could bring one out."

"I think I should be able to fit it into my busy schedule." She shot him a sideways smile. He knew how hard she'd had to work to fill her days. "I know how much he looks forward to them."

"Harold looks forward to seeing *you*," Dan said dryly.

Faith nodded. It was the truth. They'd become fast friends, and in the process she'd discovered it wasn't only women who liked to gossip.

"He likes to talk. I listen," Faith said, adding an extra teaspoonful of sugar to her coffee. She cast a sideways glance at Dan. "In fact, I heard something interesting about you."

"About me?"

"Harold says Mrs. Grosscup wanted to fix you up with her daughter but you wouldn't even give the poor girl a chance."

Dan's lips quirked at the corners. "Ever since I came back to Willow Hill from divinity school, it's been like that. Every mother or aunt sees herself as a matchmaker. It's awkward and—" a wry grin touched his lips "—sometimes downright embarrassing. You wouldn't believe some of the creative—"

"Tell me." Faith rested her elbows on the table.

"No, I don't think I'd better." He raised one hand to silence her protest. "Suffice it to say that my calling leaves me little time for romantic pursuits."

"You're not a priest."

"No, I'm not. But I believe there's a time and place for everything." He picked up his empty cup and plate and set them in the sink. "And right now, doing God's work doesn't leave much time for anything else."

Faith shrugged. He could remain single his whole life. She certainly didn't care. But the warm relaxed feeling that had penetrated her inner core only moments before had vanished, replaced by irritation.

"Sometimes God has his own agenda for us...."

Faith clapped her hands over her mouth. The words that she'd said a hundred times to her students had burst forth from her lips automatically.

Dan raised one eyebrow and an infuriating grin stole over his face. It crinkled the corners of his eyes, as if he'd been out in the sun, or smiled a lot, all his life. "Why, Faith Richards, you surprise me."

A twinge of a headache flared.

"I'm going out for a run," she said stiffly, dropping her napkin.

She pushed back her chair, the legs scraping loudly against the hardwood floor.

"Faith, wait." Dan moved quickly, halting her escape with a firm hand on her arm. "There's something I want to say. I've really enjoyed the time we've spent together."

She shivered at his nearness and swallowed hard against the sudden lump forming in her throat. "I've enjoyed it, too, Dan."

"I've always kept women at arm's length, but with you it's different."

Her heart hammered against her ribs. "It is?"

"Sure, it is." An easy smile played at the corners of his lips. "You understand my commitment to the Lord and I understand this is just a temporary stop for you. Since I don't have to worry that you're expecting more from me than friendship, I've been able to relax and be myself."

Faith raised her eyebrows. "So, in essence you're saying you don't have to worry that I'm trying to get my 'hooks' into you? Is that it?"

"Well, yes. I guess you could put it that way." Dan's tone was wary.

"I'm so glad you don't take me as a threat to your marital freedom, Pastor. Because believe me, I'm not!"

Faith summoned all her composure to walk casually from the room. Not until the door closed behind her, did hot tears sting her eyes. She blinked rapidly and brushed the wetness away with the back of her hand.

Tomorrow she'd skip breakfast and start running in the morning. Just like the pastor had said, soon she'd be gone. Riding out on that big ol' Harley, leaving Willow Hill in the dust.

It wouldn't do to get too attached to a morning ritual. Or to Daniel Whitman.

She just hoped it wasn't too late.

Tami Edwards rang the doorbell to the parsonage. She stood on her tiptoes and tried to see inside the thick lace curtains blocking the glass.

Every week she looked forward to Thursday nights. Youth Group. Dan Whitman. Could it get much better?

She'd refused Amy and Lisa's offer to walk with them. Coming early ensured she could spend some time with Pastor Dan. Alone.

Tami hugged the huge bag of popcorn to her chest and shifted impatiently from side to side. Her fingers punched the doorbell again, praying Faith Richards wouldn't be around.

Every Thursday night that had been her greatest fear. She'd even had to go to the school nurse to get something for her upset stomach. They'd attributed her stress to an upcoming test, so she'd just let them think what they wanted. She knew the real reason.

Thankfully the woman didn't seem to be into church-related activities. Someone—she forgot who—had said Faith Richards was an atheist. It sounded right to Tami, so she'd done her part to spread that rumor. And Faith's absence at church services, and even at Aunt Dora's service celebration, only served to make that explanation more plausible.

"Tami, hi." Dan opened the door and stepped aside to let her pass.

She returned his smile, noting with approval how his shirt matched his eyes. "My mother sent treats for everyone."

He took the bag of white kernels from her arms. "Great. Be sure and thank her."

Dan's hand reached around Tami, lightly touching her back as he followed her into the parlor. She shivered. The warm rich musk scent of his cologne sent her heart racing. "Are you expecting a big turnout?"

Dan set the popcorn down. "Hard to say. But I

do think we get a few more when the topic is contemporary issues.''

Tami nodded, trying to be cool. She loved it when he talked to her like an adult.

She sat down on the burgundy sofa and fingered the edge of her cardigan. ''Do you like my new sweater? I got it last week at the mall in Norfolk. Tommy Perkins says it makes my eyes look dark and mysterious.''

Dan turned slowly, his gaze glancing at the navy blue cardigan then up to the young girl's tense expression. ''It's very nice. I think Tommy Perkins is right.''

Tami breathed a sigh of relief. She'd changed four or five times before coming tonight. Thank goodness she'd picked the right outfit.

''What can I do to help?'' she asked happily.

Dan grinned, and the warmth of his smile echoed in his voice. ''You can get some bowls from the kitchen and put the popcorn around the room. They're above—''

''I know where they are,'' Tami said.

She plunged into the kitchen, then stopped abruptly. Faith Richards sat at the kitchen table painting her fingernails a deep rich crimson.

Tami hadn't really seen the woman close up, since Harvest Days. The scratch on her forehead had healed and her dark hair looked like it needed a trim. Tami fingered one of the golden locks that brushed her shoulders and wondered if men really did prefer blondes.

"Hello. It's Tami, isn't it?"

Even though Faith's words were friendly and her smile seemed genuine, Tami still hated her.

"Don't let me bother you. I'm just here to get some bowls."

"They're over the sto—"

"I know where they are. I get them all the time." Tami clipped her words. How dare this stranger act as if she lived here.

Faith's smile faded and the welcome in her eyes dimmed. "I forgot, tonight's Youth Group, isn't it?"

"You're not coming, are you?"

Faith's eyes narrowed, and Tami knew she'd heard the challenge in her voice. "No, I'm not. I'm going to paint my nails, take a bath and curl up with a book."

"You've been here a long time."

"As soon as my cycle part is in, I'll be gone."

"Good."

The door swung open and Dan stuck his head in. "Tami, are you about ready with those bowls?"

Tami flashed Faith a triumphant smile and tossed her head, her honey-colored curls cascading down her back. "Right away, Pastor Dan."

Faith watched the young girl saunter out the door and shook her head. Sometimes she really didn't miss teaching. That age could be such a challenge.

The doorbell rang continuously and sounds of teenage boys and girls filled the parlor. Faith remained in the kitchen, calmly moving from one nail to the other, applying the polish with long precise strokes.

Dan had given up asking her to help with Youth Group. In fact, he'd given up asking her to do anything. Her answer was always a firm no.

Walking out the back door to go run every morning ended up to be one of the hardest things she'd ever done. She missed his company, his conversation and his smile. But it was better this way. He'd made it clear there would never be anything more than friendship between them. After all, that's what they both wanted. Wasn't it?

"Faith." The rich baritone broke into her thoughts. Dan stood in front of her. "The hospital called. Joey's in heart failure. I need to go. Now."

"Oh, Dan."

He raked a hand through the blond curls. "I need someone to take over the Youth Group."

She shook her head. "Send them home."

Dan dropped down to his knee next to her, one hand closing over hers. "Faith, please. Do this for me. All you have to do is referee."

A trace of a smile touched her lips and he pressed on, as if sensing victory was at hand. "It's an open-topic evening. They'll just talk about some of the issues they face."

If he wouldn't have been so close, if she

wouldn't have missed him so much these past days, she might have been able to resist. She took a deep breath, knowing she'd regret her words, but wanting so much to please him. "Okay, I'll do it."

"That's my girl." His hands grasped her shoulders giving her a quick squeeze.

"I wish," she said softly to herself.

Faith walked into the parlor and conversation ceased. Feeling like Daniel entering the lion's den, she pasted a smile on her face and sat down.

She'd barely gotten settled when Tami announced she'd been chosen to pick the evening's topic. With a smug smile the girl stood, looking like an angel with her blond hair billowing around her face, the color of her sweater emphasizing her huge blue eyes. "Tonight the topic is premarital sex."

The boys perked up and the girls blushed. Faith groaned to herself.

"Miss Richards. How 'bout we go around the room and have everyone share if they'd ever lusted after anyone."

The girls tittered and one boy sought center stage with a joke about "How do you know if it's lust or love?"

Faith stopped the joke midsentence with her best withering glance, but Tami didn't miss a beat. The girl batted her long lashes and leaned back against Tommy Perkins. "Maybe it would be helpful if you discussed virginity from your own perspective. Unless that's not possible...."

"Tami, I—"

"Okay, let's just say you've done something you regret. What does God say about that?" Tami interrupted, her eyes wide and innocent.

Faith hesitated. The girl was much too young to have such regrets. Still, such things were not impossible. "God's word is clear. There are no sins that He cannot cleanse. Open your Bibles to *Psalms* 103:9-12."

The shuffle of Bible pages followed her request. After reading the passage out loud, Faith smiled at the intent young faces in front of her. "It's never too late to change your ways and travel down the godly path."

She made some important points to close, all the while encouraging the youth to discuss their concerns with their parents.

They filed out, laughing and whispering. A few of them stopped to thank her. Despite some rocky moments, she'd realized she might have learned more than they had. Leading the discussion made her realize how much she missed teaching.

Tami lingered in the foyer for the longest while.

"Are you waiting for someone? Do you need a ride home?" Faith asked.

"No, I needed to talk to Pastor Dan. I thought he'd be home by now."

"I could give him a message...."

The young girl's eyes hardened. "No, I'll talk to him another time."

The teen couldn't leave quickly enough. As she turned the corner, Faith's brows drew together. Tami'd been so friendly when they'd first met. What had changed?

The girl had barely disappeared from sight when the pickup's headlights swung into the drive. Faith stood in the doorway and waited.

When she saw Dan's expression, she was glad all the kids had gone on.

"What happened?"

Dan wiped a weary hand across his eyes. A day's growth of beard stubbled his square jaw and his blue eyes were troubled. "Oh, Faith, he's doing so bad."

Her desire to comfort him made her forget the tension between them. She caressed his cheek, the skin cold beneath her fingertips. He reached out and caught her hand in his, lacing his fingers with her own. Their gazes locked.

Then, oh so naturally, his hands slipped up her arms, bringing her closer. She hugged his neck, drawing him to her, feeling the ache in his heart, the pain in his soul. She buried her face against his chest.

She held him. He held her. Reveling in the comfort of each other's caring. Drawing strength from the nearness.

Faith couldn't say when that changed. It just seemed so right to raise her face to his and feel his soft breath fan her cheeks.

His lips slowly descended to meet hers and she kissed him gently, savoring the moment. Raising his mouth from hers, Dan gazed into her eyes and lightly fingered a loose tendril of hair.

"My sweet Faith," he whispered.

Her pulse skittered alarmingly at the soft brushing of his fingers against her face. She raised her gaze. Was the light flickering in his blue depths merely a reflection of her own need?

Dan kissed her again.

She returned his kiss, her fingers running through his hair.

He whispered her name, his breath soft against her ear. But when he murmured, his voice unsteady, "We need to stop," her heart rebelled. She held him even tighter.

He stepped back from her arms, his uneven breathing telling her the effort it took.

She trembled, and her hands fluttered to her hair. She could feel the warmth rise up her neck.

Awkwardly she cleared her throat. "It's getting late. I guess I'll go to bed."

His eyes darkened with emotion and he studied her face with his enigmatic glance for an extra beat. "Good night Faith."

Faith climbed the stairs without a backward glance. If she had looked back, she would have seen what Tami saw through the front window: the light of love shining strong in the preacher's blue eyes as he stood staring, watching her disappear from view.

Chapter Twelve

Faith pulled her gaze from the ceiling and closed her eyes. She'd been awake since dawn, her mind and heart racing at breakneck speed, and all because of one unexpected kiss.

She touched her lips and her breath caught in her throat. The first kiss had been good. The warm sweetness of the second had been even better. What would a third kiss bring?

Faith sighed, refusing to torment herself with such speculations. There wouldn't be any more kisses to compare, not when she and Dan both knew there could never be anything between them.

So what? a tiny voice inside whispered. You like him. What's wrong with a few friendly kisses? Faith paused and considered the possibilities.

She'd lived her whole life following someone

else's rules, and where had it gotten her? Accused of something she didn't do, out of a job and all alone in the world. In the great scheme of things, a little recreational kissing had to be far down on anyone's list of don'ts. They were both adults. She'd be leaving soon anyway. Who would be hurt?

Faith ignored the warnings she'd given the teenagers last night and pushed aside the nagging knowledge that *she* would be the one hurt when it came time for her to leave. Dan would still have what mattered most to him: his God and his church.

The sound of voices wafted up through the floorboards—a deep masculine one laughing, a feminine one talking. Faith propped herself up on her elbows and listened intently, unable to catch more than a few words. The conversation quickly ceased, replaced by heavy footsteps moving through the downstairs. The closet door in the foyer opened then slammed shut.

Faith threw back the bedcovers and sprang from the bed. Suddenly, inexplicably, she needed to see him again. She peeled off the sweatpants and T-shirt she used for pajamas and replaced them with a ragged pair of jeans and a bulky sweater that hung to her knees. She raced down the hall, her feet swift on the hardwood floor.

The front door creaked open, and like a sprinter trying to beat the clock, Faith took the stairs two at a time. She arrived at the bottom in record time.

"Dan." Her chest rose and fell beneath the thick cable knit, her breath coming in short quick puffs.

"Faith, I didn't expect to see you up so early." His brow furrowed in concern. "Is something wrong?"

"Wrong?" She brushed a stray strand of hair from her face and feigned an air of nonchalance. "What makes you think something's wrong?"

"Oh, I don't know. Maybe 'cause you practically flew down those last few steps." A smile tugged at his lips, "Or maybe 'cause you've got that I-just-jumped-out-of-bed look going."

Faith cast a sideways glance at the beveled mirror on the wall and grimaced. Cowlicks stood every way but down. She resisted the almost overpowering urge to spit and smooth. Instead she raised her chin and shot him her best saucy smile. "Thanks for the compliment."

His dimples flashed. "Your sweater is on inside out."

She didn't even look down. "It's the style."

"And the bare feet?" His gaze lingered on her brightly painted toenails and her breathing sped up again.

"Completes the fashion statement," she said.

He grinned. "It does send a certain message."

The grandfather clock chimed. Dan's gaze jerked to the dial. "And that's sending me another message. I better get going or I'm going to be late."

He turned on his heel, but she grabbed his sleeve,

strangely reluctant to see him go. "I wanted to talk to you about last night."

He hesitated. "So you've been thinking about what happened, too."

"I haven't thought of much else," Faith said with honest candor.

"Last night when I came home…" His eyes softened and her breath caught in her throat. He took her hand. "It meant a lot to have you here waiting."

A sweet tenderness flowed like warm honey up her arm. An answering affection flared in his eyes and boosted her courage.

She took a step forward.

"Faith." He cleared his throat, but she paid no attention. "I don't think…"

One more step and she stood so close, his heat mingled with hers. So close, it took no effort at all to raise her hand and lay it against his cheek. So close, she swore she could hear the beating of his heart.

"Last night—" she said softly "—meant a lot to me, too."

He swallowed hard and she held her breath in anticipation. She ignored everything else: the ringing of the phone, a faraway voice. All that mattered was Dan Whitman and right now.

His hand rose to cup her face and his mouth lowered to meet hers. Her fingers parted his hair and she pulled him even closer. The clatter of heels on the hardwood floor matched the cadence of her heart.

"Pastor Dan." Dora's voice rang out.

They jerked apart.

"I'm glad I caught..." Dora's voice and steps stopped at the same time. Her gaze shifted from Dan to Faith. "I'm sorry, I didn't mean to interrupt...."

Faith smoothed her hair and surveyed Dora with a critical eye. Regardless of what the older woman said, Faith concluded Dora looked decidedly more amused than sorry.

"No problem," Dan said a little too quickly. "I was just telling Faith I needed to get to the church."

"Is that what you were telling her?" A momentary twinkle danced in Dora's pale eyes. "Anyway, there's no need for you to rush off. Mr. Cameron just called. Your meeting has been canceled."

"It has?"

"Indeed," Dora said with an emphatic nod. "Maybe now you'll be able to take some time for breakfast. I'm sure you must be hungry."

Faith resisted the urge to steal a glance at Dan. She'd bet anything he was hungry all right, but not for bacon and eggs. "I'll be glad to make us all something."

"Oh, none for me, my dear. I've already eaten." Dora waved a hand breezily. "I'm off to the store."

"This early?" Dan said, raising a brow.

"Beat the crowds," Dora said.

Faith's admiration for the older woman grew. How she could possibly keep a straight face when spouting such nonsense showed true talent. Every time Faith had been to the A & P, the staff had outnumbered customers two to one. Faith suspected the only reason the store opened early was to capture the doughnuts and soft drink business of a handful of teenagers on their way to school.

Dan paused, his gaze still puzzled. "But I thought you just went to the supermarket yesterday."

"You're so right." Dora's laugh trilled. "But I forgot the bread."

Faith could have pointed out she'd personally unloaded three loaves from the grocery sacks, but she remained silent and Dora bustled out, a satisfied smile on her face.

"Well." Faith waited until she heard the front door shut before she turned back to Dan, her lips already tingling in anticipation. "Where were we?"

"Headed down the wrong road. Again." Dan's gaze met hers and his voice filled with the same regret she'd seen in his eyes last night. "I'm beginning to think it's not such a good idea for us to be alone together."

"Evidently Aunt Dora doesn't think so," Faith pointed out.

He rocked back on his heels and blew out a harsh breath.

"Don't you want to kiss me?" she pressed on, unwilling to concede defeat.

"Of course." He raked his fingers through his hair. "Too much."

Encouraged, she took a deep breath and continued boldly. "So what's the problem?"

"I'm a minister, Faith."

"I hate to tell you, Dan, but that's old news." She flashed him a teasing smile.

He rubbed the back of his neck with one hand. "As Christians, we have to avoid putting ourselves in positions where we can be tempted."

Since when had he gotten so stuffy? "Well, I'm *not* a Christian." *Not anymore.*

"That brings up another point." His expression turned solemn and his gaze sought hers. "I'm a Christian. You're not. There can never be anything between you and me, Faith. We're just too different."

She dropped her lashes quickly to hide the hurt. He'd offered the words matter-of-factly, stating what must seem to him to be an obvious truth.

But it's not true, we're not that different, she wanted to say. We both believe in treating people the way we'd like to be treated, we both love animals and children. Instead she kept silent, knowing deep down in the one way that truly mattered they *were* worlds apart.

"Faith, I didn't mean to hurt you...."

His words echoed in her head, rousing her tattered pride. She straightened and considered the merits of lying.

"Oh, Dan, don't be silly. I'd certainly never planned on anything between us." Faith gave a little laugh as if the thought was too ridiculous to even contemplate further.

"I do like you, Faith. And—" his voice was smooth and controlled, but she sensed the emotion churning beneath the surface "—I think you like me, too."

She forced a bright smile despite the sudden lump in her throat. "You're okay."

He chuckled.

"Different though we are, I think we can both agree that—" a trace of a smile touched his lips "—because of this crazy chemistry between us, we'd better keep our time alone to a minimum."

Faith heaved a heartfelt sigh. What he said made perfect sense. How could she argue with logic? With his granite resolve, it would just be an effort in futility anyway. She almost had to laugh. Here she'd finally convinced herself casual kissing would be okay, and now her partner fizzled out, apparently afraid of where it might lead.

But then, what should she have expected? He was above all a minister. A man committed to traveling the straight and narrow. If she wanted to take a side road, she'd have to find someone else to go there with her. A man who would be more interested in the here and now rather than the hereafter.

Chapter Thirteen

Keeping their distance might have been easier these past three days, Faith reflected, if they weren't living under the same roof. And if she only knew what it was she really wanted.

She glanced at Dan across the breakfast table and took a bite of toast. Until her bike was up and running, she was in a holding pattern with nothing to do, and now, no one to take up her time.

"More coffee, Faith?" Aunt Dora lifted the carafe from the lazy Susan.

Faith smiled a refusal. Of course she could always join Aunt Dora and her quilting club. But then she'd never been much of a seamstress, and just the idea of wasting what promised to be a beautiful fall day went against her grain.

"What are your plans today, *Pastor?*"

Dan raised a brow and set his coffee cup on the table. Out of necessity, she'd started addressing him as Pastor. She needed some way to remind herself why he was so wrong for her.

His thumb rubbed the rim of his mug. "I'll be at the church. I have a sermon that's giving me some trouble."

"Tsk-tsk." Aunt Dora shook her head. "You shouldn't be stuck inside on such a beautiful day. You should be out enjoying God's splendor."

Faith shot Dora an amused glance. Obviously the woman had forgotten her own plans to be indoors all day.

"I agree, Dora." Faith stood and stretched. "Winter will be here before we know it. I just hope I'm long gone before then."

A pained expression crossed the matriarch's face. Dan remained silent.

"I've got an idea." Dora's face brightened. "Why don't you and Pastor Dan take advantage of the day and have a picnic lunch? I'd be glad to pack a basket."

Faith could almost hear Dan groan. She flashed him a smile and tilted her head expectantly, even though she didn't believe for one second he'd agree.

"I'd like to, Dora, but I really need to finish this sermon."

Faith chuckled and shook her head. The man was so transparent.

Dan cast her a warning glance.

"Coward," she mouthed when Dora turned toward the sink.

"I am—" Dan said out loud before stopping himself.

"Did you say something?" Dora swiveled and cast Dan a questioning glance.

Dan cleared his throat and reached for the carafe. "I said I think I will have some more coffee."

"You know a picnic does sound like fun," Faith said, realizing it might be just the thing to pull her out of her blue funk. "Why don't *you* join me, Dora?"

"I would, honey, but my quilting circle..."

Ugh. The dreaded quilting circle. "That's right. For a second it slipped my mind. I guess this will have to be a picnic for one." Her gaze shifted to Dan, who shoveled cereal into his mouth with extra vigor. "Unless I can get you to change your mind?"

"I said no," he snapped without even looking up.

"Daniel—" Dora swiveled, her brows drawn in censure "—there's no reason to be so short. Faith was just asking."

"Sorry." Dan's apology and smile may have convinced Dora but the look he shot Faith told a different story. He shoved back his chair. "I need to get going."

"Are you sure?" she said.

"Very sure." The sunlight from the window reflected off his hair, glinting gold. His eyes shone a clear porcelain blue, a deep resolve reflected in their depths.

"Well—" she rose and waved her hand loosely "—if you change your mind about the picnic, I'll be at the gazebo south of the lake."

"I won't."

She smiled and shrugged. He might make her wait, but he'd be there. The look in his eyes guaranteed it.

A smatter of laughter and the pungent aroma of wood smoke wafted up from the bonfire down by the lake. Faith stood perfectly still with the memory of another picnic when the air had been filled with a natural gaiety and the smell of a campfire.

It had been late fall and her parents were leaving for Africa the next day. The picnic at a favorite park would be their going-away party. They'd had a grand time, stuffing themselves with hot dogs, potato salad and chips before moving on to the gourmet dessert they all loved: s'mores. Her father cut the sticks from tree branches and the three of them impatiently toasted marshmallows over the open flame, preparing them for the little sandwiches of chocolate and graham crackers carefully laid out on the red-checked tablecloth. She and her father had carefully turned their marshmallows a lovely golden brown, but her mother had burnt hers black, insisting it made the melted gooey inside extra-sweet.

The pain of their deaths slammed into her with gale wind force, perhaps because it had been almost a year to the day that her parents' plane had crashed. Faith squeezed her eyes shut to stop the tears filling her eyes. Hadn't she already cried a bucketfull of tears? And had it changed anything? They were still gone and she was still here: three hundred pages into *War and Peace,* and never more alone.

Anger flooded her. She'd been so sure he'd come.

The sun dropped another notch in the western sky and she pulled on her jacket against the increasingly brisk north wind.

"Faith."

Her pulse quickened and she set the basket back down on the picnic table and turned, a relieved smile lifting her lips. "Dan, I won—"

The words lodged in her throat. He'd come all right, dressed for a picnic in blue jeans and a sweatshirt. But he hadn't come alone.

"Tami…Amy," Faith said through a frozen smile and clenched teeth. "What a nice surprise."

The girls wore matching school jackets and the same petulant expressions. Clearly they were no more glad to see her than she was to see them.

Only when Dan shifted his gaze to the girls did Tami shoot Faith a phony smile. Amy followed with a small, tentative one, only slightly more sincere.

Dan appeared not to notice the tension permeating the gazebo. He plopped down on the bench and picked up her book.

"Tolstoy?" He gave her a sidelong glance of utter disbelief. "Tell me you didn't read this much today?"

Faith smiled faintly. What did he expect? She'd been waiting most of the day with nothing better to do. "I had the time and it's a great story."

Amy shook her head. "I couldn't even make it past the first chapter when we had it in World Lit."

"When we have extra time at my house we read the Bible," Tami said, tossing a strand of hair over her shoulder.

"No way," Amy said, suppressing a giggle.

Tami jabbed her friend in the ribs.

Dan set the heavy novel back on the table. "Your father always has made studying the Scriptures a priority."

Tami flushed with pleasure at Dan's approving smile.

"Do you read the Bible, Miss Richards?" Tami said, casting a look at Dan to make sure he was listening.

Faith thought back to the years of church school, of the evening devotions with her family, the Bible study lessons she'd hosted in her home. She thought of her parents. "No, I don't. It's a waste of time."

"Faith," Dan said sharply, his gaze shifting pointedly to the girls.

"But, Miss Richards—" Tami's shocked expression didn't fool Faith for a minute "—you led our Bible study the other night."

Faith paused. The words she'd read had stirred her soul in ways she didn't want to remember. "I could lead a discussion on Karl Marx and his beliefs but that wouldn't mean I was a Communist, would it?"

"I knew it," Tami said, triumphantly turning to Amy. "Didn't I tell you she was an atheist!"

"Girls." A tiny muscle twitched in Dan's jaw. "It's getting late. I think it's time you joined the others down by the lake."

Tami hesitated. Her gaze lingered on Dan and the irritation that colored his features. A smile of satisfaction lifted her lips. "C'mon, Amy. Let's go."

Dan waited until the two were out of sight before he spoke. "Do you mind telling me what that was all about?"

"If you don't mind telling me what took you so long to get here." Faith shoved the rest of her items into the basket with unnecessary force and whirled to face him.

"I never said I'd come."

"No, but we both knew that you would, didn't we?" She lifted her chin and fixed her gaze.

Dan's jaw tightened. "I shouldn't even be here."

"Then, why are you?"

"Amy's parents are having a cookout down by the lake. I agreed to bring out the four who had to stay late at school."

"The Good Samaritan strikes again," she said with a trace of bitterness.

"It gave me a good excuse to see you without..." He stopped and took a breath.

"Without what? Being alone with me? That's what you were going to say, wasn't it?" She shook her head in disgust. "Tell me something, Dan. Why don't you really want to be alone with me? Because I want to kiss *you?* Or is it because *you* want to kiss *me?*"

"Faith—" Dan leaned forward against the table, his hands clenching the edge so tightly his knuckles turned white "—try to understand...."

"I understand only too well." Faith zipped her coat with a single jerk.

"What is it you want from me?" He shoved his hand through his hair in frustration and a spike stuck up on one side.

"Nothing," she said, suddenly realizing it was true. She didn't need any more heartache, and that's what she'd get from a relationship with Dan Whitman. "Absolutely nothing."

He watched her gather her things, a troubled expression on his face. "Sometimes I don't think I know you at all."

"You don't," she said matter-of-factly. "You

may be attracted to me. But despite what you say, you don't particularly like me and you certainly can't begin to understand where I'm coming from."

"You're so very wrong," he said softly.

"Don't worry about it, Pastor. I'm a big girl. None of it matters. I don't need you or your God to be happy."

"We all need someone, Faith. And everybody needs God."

"Not me. Not anymore." She tossed the leftover chicken salad sandwich and the rest of the potato salad into the trash. "Of course I could have used someone to have lunch with earlier today, but I certainly didn't *need* anyone."

A shriek of laughter down by the lake punctuated her words.

"You'd better go rescue the parents," Faith said. "Sounds like the natives are getting wild."

"Faith, I'm sorry...."

"I'm sorry, too. I thought we could be friends. I guess I was mistaken." Faith glanced down the road and calculated how long it would take her to walk back. "I need to get going."

"I'll take you back to the parsonage."

"Forget it."

"Get in the truck."

She raised a brow. "Trying the forceful approach?"

"Just get in the truck. You're not walking."

"I'll be fine." She shot him a smile as phony as

the one Tami had given her earlier. "After all, if we're alone I might not be able to control myself. I wouldn't want to put you in any danger."

His lips twitched. "Okay, I deserved that. But you're still not walking home."

Home. She didn't have a home. Not anymore. She gazed into Dan's hopeful expression. What did it matter if she walked or rode? For that matter, what did anything matter?

"Make yourself useful." Faith shoved the picnic basket into Dan's hands and walked toward the truck.

Chapter Fourteen

Faith ignored the whispers. Today of all days she needed to be here. She lifted her chin and slipped into a seat by the aisle. Aunt Dora's face lit with surprise and pleasure from a pew a few rows away.

The past few days she'd done a lot of thinking. About her life. About her faith. And about Dan Whitman. Her gaze shifted to the front.

Sunlight streamed in from the stained-glass windows. Rays of sparkling gold reflected off Dan's carefully combed hair. The smile he flashed toward the congregation glowed and Faith basked in its warmth.

''Mornin', Miss Faith. Ain't seen you here before.''

Shivers rippled down Faith's spine at the familiar voice. In horror, she turned. Hank Lundegard shot her an oily grin.

"Hank," she finally managed to spit out, "what are you doing here?"

"Why, I come to hear my sins are forgiven." He winked. "Same as you."

Faith glanced around, frantically searching for another place to sit.

"No need to look any further, missy. It's plumb full. Most of the folks are here 'cause their kids made 'em come. They're singin' today. My Lisa—" his thumb jerked in the direction of the youth choir sitting in front "—is the tall one in the back row."

Faith wanted to point out most of those in attendance were there to hear the Lord's word, but she kept quiet. She had too much else to deal with.

The first hymn started and Hank held out the book for her to share. When Dan read the epistle, Hank yawned and drew caricatures of women on the back of the church bulletin.

Faith concentrated on the service and desperately tried to ignore the man at her side.

His hand dropped to rest lightly on her knee.

She froze.

One arm snaked around her shoulders to rest on the back of the pew.

Her stomach churned.

Dan's strong, confident voice faltered but Faith barely noticed, the memory of another man and another time flooding her consciousness.

The minute the service ended, she vaulted from

her seat. She brushed past the line waiting to shake Dan's hand and headed for the exit.

By the time Dan arrived home, her emotions were at the breaking point. She didn't even give him a second glance when he strolled into the parlor, a tray of sandwiches and a glass of milk in his hands.

Dan set the food on the coffee table and plopped down on the sofa. "Aunt Dora went over to Ray's for lunch so we have to fend for ourselves."

Faith shook her head. "Thanks, but I'm not really hungry."

Dan leaned forward. His elbows rested on his knees. "What's the matter, Faith? I can tell something's troubling you. If you feel like talking, I'm a good listener."

For a long moment she hesitated. A sigh escaped her throat. "My parents died a year ago today."

"I'm sorry, I didn't know."

She took a deep breath and continued as if he hadn't even spoken. "Being in church brought back a lot of memories. We—we used to always attend services together."

Faith knew if she closed her eyes she'd see them as they'd looked the last Sunday before they'd left for the mission fields: her mother's ash-blond hair pulled back in a loose chignon, that perpetual smile on her lips, her father wearing the blue-and-red striped tie she'd given him for Father's Day, holding his leather-bound Bible in his hands.

She kept her gaze focused ahead and her eyes wide open.

"What happened?"

A tight fist of guilt gripped her heart.

"Their plane went down over the ocean. It was the first crash for that South African airline. They told me that when they called." She gave a little laugh. "Can you believe it? I never could figure out why they said that. What did it matter if they'd never lost a plane before? My parents were dead, as was everyone else on board."

Dan frowned. "I think I remember reading about that accident. Wasn't it some sort of freak storm off the coast of—"

"You have a good memory. I don't even know if I'd have noticed."

"I probably wouldn't have, either, but there was an article about two of the passengers in our church journal. They were Bible translators and had been working with an incredibly difficult African dialect."

"Those were my parents."

Dan's eyes widened. "But you said you weren't even a Christian."

"They were the ones doing the church work, not me," she pointed out.

"Still—" Dan's brows knit together "—you would have grown up in the faith, so—"

"Stop right there." Faith's voice lowered, tight and controlled. "I know where you're heading. You think I turned my back on God because of my parents' deaths. But it's just not that simple."

"Then tell me the complicated version."

"It would take all afternoon." She grabbed a sandwich from the plate.

Dan waited until she had taken a few bites and accepted a sip of his milk before he probed further. "Tell me, Faith."

She swallowed hard against the lump in her throat. "They left for Africa when I graduated from college. I was an only child and they weren't just my parents, they were my friends.

"They were only on that flight because I asked them to come." She furiously blinked back the tears. "I was having sort of a rough time of it...."

I couldn't handle my own problems. If it weren't for their weak, selfish daughter they never would have been on that plane.

For a moment she feared she'd spoken aloud. But then she realized it would be derision she'd see reflected in those blue eyes, not understanding.

Dan reached over and patted her hand. "Faith, sweetheart, I'm sure they wanted to be with you."

She sniffed and brushed the tears back with her sleeve. "It doesn't matter. I lost my parents. I lost my job. Even God deserted me."

The glow from the fire cast shadows against the walls, and only the ticking from the grandfather clock broke the silence.

"Deserted you?"

The bitterness welled inside. All too vividly she recalled those terrible days when her world had crumbled around her like shifting sand. There'd been no solid rock to cling to; even God had forsaken her. Her prayers had gone unanswered. "I'd spent my life worshiping someone who didn't lift a finger to help me when I needed Him the most."

Dan shifted his body forward, and even in the dim light his eyes shone with an inner glow. "God never deserted you, Faith. He may not have answered your prayers the way you thought they should be answered, but I guarantee He has been there—right beside you—every step of the way."

He reached for the Bible on the end table, thumbing through the well-worn pages, "Listen to the words of Paul. 'I can do everything through Him who gives me strength.'"

He shut the book and gazed at her thoughtfully. "Through difficulties we learn to rely on the Lord even more. We can't trust in the things of this world, but we can trust in Him. Our strength flows from Him."

"I don't know...." She desperately wanted to believe, but how could she, after all that had happened?

"Pray, Faith. His grace is sufficient for you. Let Him be strong for you."

Dan blanketed her hand with his and said a quick prayer.

Tears stung her lids. She rose from the chair and

swallowed against the lump in her throat. "You've chosen the right profession, Daniel Whitman."

He laid his arm around her shoulder and walked with her to the stairs. "It's not a job to me."

Faith started up the stairs, then stopped and turned back to him. Putting her hands on his arm, she rose on tiptoe to give him a light kiss on the cheek. "Thank you."

Dan sighed deeply. Her stay in Willow Hill had God's handiwork written all over it. Why had he not seen it before? With Him at her side Faith would be able to face her fears and get on with her life. Move on. And wasn't that exactly what he was supposed to do as a minister? Then why did it bother him so much?

He'd dedicated his life to Christ's mission and couldn't afford to be distracted by romantic notions. Maybe in a few years, when he had more time....

She'll be long gone by then.

Taking a deep breath, Dan shoved the thought aside and reached for his Bible. Despite his attraction, his ministry came first. And romance... Well, it would just have to wait.

"Did you see her?" Although they were the only ones remaining in the sanctuary, Amy spoke in a hushed whisper. The church had emptied immediately after the service, but the three girls had lingered.

"I saw her all right." Tami's heart tightened and

the unexpected pressure made it hurt to breathe, much less talk. "Since when do atheists go to church?"

"This is the first time I've seen her here." Lisa picked at a ragged cuticle with her fingernail. "I kind of liked her red dress."

"Lisa." Amy's voice rang with disapproval.

"Well, it *was* cute," Lisa said, flinging a strand of hair over her shoulder. "A little too long, but still—"

"Lisa," Tami said sharply. "Forget the dress."

"Yeah, forget the dress," Amy echoed loyally.

"I noticed she was sitting next to your dad." Tami couldn't quite keep the hope from her voice. "Are they back together?"

"He hasn't seen her since that night." Lisa's gaze shifted from her cuticle to rest speculatively on Tami. "You look worried. You don't think there's something going on between her and Pastor Dan, do you?"

Just hearing her worst fear spoken sent a chill down Tami's spine. Since the night of Youth Group, she'd been unable to banish the picture of the two of them enfolded in each other's arms. When she closed her eyes to sleep, when she let her mind wander, and today when she'd seen Faith Richards in church gazing at Pastor Dan with that lovestruck expression, the sickening image had returned in full vivid color.

Tami pushed up from the pew, unable to sit any

longer. She lifted her face and gazed up at the stained glass, the light from sun shining through it warming her face. "Remember the story of Jezebel?"

Lisa tilted her head questioningly and Amy frowned as if trying to remember. Tami shook her head. Was she the only one who listened in Sunday school?

"Forget it." Tami waved her hand dismissively. "The point is Faith Richards is bad news. She's no good for Pastor Dan. Or for Willow Hill, either."

Lisa rose slowly from her seat and stretched. "The question is—what are you going to do about it?"

"Tami's got a plan," Amy said, her flashing eyes daring Lisa to disagree. "She always has a plan."

Tami smiled a bright confident smile that seemed to fool her friends. Like robbers planning a heist, the girls leaned closer, glancing around to make sure no one was listening.

Tami lowered her voice, just in case. "First, I'm going to work even harder to get Pastor Dan to notice me."

"Good idea." Lisa nodded approvingly. "Make him jealous. My dad says it works every time."

"It does?" Tami said in surprise.

"Sure," Lisa said, warming to the subject. "If there's some chick he wants, he always makes sure he mentions how many other women are hot after him. He says that if a woman thinks someone wants you, it just makes them want you more."

"Makes sense." Tami looked at Lisa admiringly. Who would have ever thought Hank would have such good advice?

"What else are you going to do?" Lisa asked.

Tami thought for a minute. "Tommy's dad works at the garage. I'm going to find out why that Harley isn't done yet."

Amy spoke quickly, as if determined to get her two cents' worth in. "Yeah, if you can get that motorcycle fixed, she'll have no excuse to stay."

If only she could be so sure, Tami thought. The way Pastor Dan and Faith Richards had looked at each other today told her it might not be that simple.

Chapter Fifteen

❧

Faith bounded down the stairs to the kitchen. The smell of bacon and eggs greeted her. Today she'd awakened, anxious for the day to begin.

"Good morning, everyone." Faith couldn't keep the grin from her face.

"My, my. Someone certainly got up on the right side of the bed this morning." Aunt Dora glanced up from sputtering bacon.

"Good morning, Faith," Dan said.

Faith threw him an even more dazzling smile and plopped into the wooden chair. "Isn't it a wonderful day?"

Buoyed by hope and optimism, even the gray skies outside couldn't dull her spirits. Last night she'd reflected on the past, on the future and on what Dan had said. For the first time in months, she'd picked up a Bible. Familiar words she'd read all her life came alive in a new way.

Finally she'd dropped to her knees and prayed. Shortly before midnight, she found the peace that for so long had eluded her, rediscovering her Lord in the process. Now she stood ready to face life, with an unbeatable ally at her side.

Aunt Dora brushed the lace curtains back with one bony finger. "It's cloudy and only supposed to reach fifty degrees."

"Still, we're alive, we have our health."

Dan chuckled. "Dora, I think Faith is right. Let's rejoice in this day the Lord has made."

Aunt Dora shook her head, a smile tugging at her lips. "Very well, but I'm going to see if you two are still saying that when it's twenty below."

Faith exchanged a smile with Dan and reached for a piece of toast. She buttered it lavishly, reveling in the rich thickness of the pure butter, the texture of the dense wheat bread. Even the juice in her glass seemed to sparkle, the bits of pulp highlighting the pure orange smoothness.

"Here's your bacon and eggs, and I don't want to hear any comments about cholesterol or calories. It wouldn't hurt you to put a little meat on those bones," announced Aunt Dora.

Faith glanced down. Always slender, her blue jeans now hung loose and baggy around her legs. The red sweatshirt that Dan had loaned her, sat large and bulky around her thin frame.

"You're right. I'm scrawny as a plucked chicken." She added an extra dollop of cream to her coffee.

"Oh, I wouldn't say that," Dan said, a bemused smile on his face.

"Oh, you wouldn't, would you?" She caught a glimpse of the flickering flame in his eyes. The laughter died in her throat.

"I'm off. The altar society is meeting at nine." Aunt Dora glanced knowingly at the two of them. She smiled and untied her apron. "Dan, keep our guest company while she eats. I'll tell the office you might be a few minutes late."

The older woman bustled out of the kitchen and a wave of shyness swept over Faith. She raised the juice glass, took a sip and searched for a safe topic. "I want to thank you for yesterday afternoon."

"Thank me?"

"For taking time to listen." She reached across the table and blanketed his hand with hers. Instantly she realized her mistake. She pulled her hand back, her thoughts a jumbled mess.

"If there's ever anything else I can do…"

You could kiss me.

Faith flushed and forced her gaze from his lips. Talk about physical attraction. It didn't just happen to teens.

The image of Tami Edwards broke the spell.

She hesitated. "Dan, there's something I need to

tell you. It's about what was said during our Youth Group discussion.''

Dan reached for the carafe of coffee. He raised the pot and she shook her head. He poured himself another cup.

"Let me remember, the discussion topic was—" his brows drew together in thought "—serving others."

"Serving others?"

"That was supposed to be the topic. What did you talk about?"

"Premarital sex."

Dan choked on his coffee. "You're kidding me."

Faith shook her head, her heart sinking.

"I mean, that's fine, but if you don't mind my asking, why did you tackle such a hard subject?"

"Tami Edwards wanted to discuss it."

"Tami?" Dan's gaze grew thoughtful. "Really?"

"That's what I wanted to talk to you about." Faith leaned forward and rested her arms on the table. "When we started discussing love versus lust and regrets, I got the distinct feeling that Tami may have done something she regretted. Dan, she's only a child."

"That surprises me."

"I know, but we both realize how strong those drives can be."

His eyes shone with an inner light and he nodded. "Yes, we do."

"The first time I met her she was going on and on about this really cool guy she liked. I noticed at the meeting she sat awfully close to Tommy Perkins." She hesitated, not sure how much to elaborate. "I think picking that discussion topic may have been a cry for help."

Dan slowly sipped his coffee. "You could be right."

"And she certainly seems to come over a lot. Maybe she's been trying to find an opportunity to talk to you alone."

"That could be true." He rubbed his chin thoughtfully. "Her father's sending her over with some financial papers. I'm definitely going to make sure we have time to talk. Today."

Tami Edwards hurried down the sidewalk to the parsonage. The crisp northern wind stung her cheeks but she scarcely noticed. Anticipation propelled her down the block. Aunt Dora shouldn't be around. Her church circle met today.

Tami bounded up the front steps. Dan opened the door with a big smile of welcome.

They finalized plans for the Youth Group lock-in. For once the pastor didn't seem in a hurry. They chatted over brownies and milk, and Tami made sure she mentioned several times how popular she was with the other kids.

"I imagine someone as pretty as you has to fight the boys off," Dan said.

Tami flashed him a big smile, glad he'd gotten her point. Lisa said it never hurt to make the one you love jealous. "Tommy Perkins—you know he's a junior and captain of the football team—he says I'm the prettiest girl in the whole school."

"So—" Dan leaned back in his chair and laced his fingers together "—do you and Tommy go out?"

Tami gloried in the moment. He *was* jealous!

She smiled and nodded, batting her double-mascara-coated lashes at him. No need for him to know that her parents wouldn't allow her to date yet. It made her sound like such a baby.

"Tami."

The way he said her name sent shivers up her spine. She leaned forward. "Yes, Pastor Dan?"

"I want you to know that you can talk to me about anything. That's what I'm here for. I realize some things are harder to talk about than others."

Had he guessed her true feelings? Her face warmed at the thought.

Dan's eyes softened. "Faith told me about the other night at Youth Group."

Faith. The hair on the back of her neck bristled. "What did *she* say?"

"She said the discussion centered around pre-marital sex and you expressed some regrets—"

Hot fire scorched her veins. Tami shoved back the chair and jerked to her feet. "She said what!"

"Tami, God loves you. If you and Tommy have done some things that you shouldn't—"

"Don't!" Her blood pounded so hard, she thought for a moment if he said another word she would faint. She grasped the top of the chair for support. That lying Faith. "I have not done anything with Tommy Perkins." She choked out the words, unable to believe they were having this discussion. "Or with any other boy."

"Tami..."

She turned away from the disappointment she saw reflected in his blue eyes. How dare Faith Richards make up those lies, when she was the one fooling around with Hank Lundegard and—Tami swallowed hard against the memory—Pastor Dan himself.

She'd be sorry.

Tami took a deep breath and grabbed her bag. "I need to get going. My mother's expecting me."

"I didn't mean to upset you. If you ever need to talk..."

Her feet fairly flew out of the house. She never looked back. By the time she reached her front door she knew what must be done.

She pushed open the heavy oak door. The shiny wood floors gleamed. Her stomach churned at the aroma of freshly baked cookies coming from the kitchen.

"Tami, is that you? Come and join me in the kitchen, I just made some chocolate-chip cookies."

"In a minute, Mom."

Squaring her shoulders, she took a deep breath and cracked the door to the den. "Dad, can I talk to you a minute? It's important."

The stress of the past hour must have shown on her face because he pushed the laptop aside, immediately giving her his full attention.

"I always have time for my princess."

At any other time she would have smiled at the endearment. The youngest of four children and the only girl, she reveled in her favored status. Her father had always put her on a pedestal, and in return she let him think she was perfect.

What would happen if that lying Faith went to him with her suspicions? Just like she had Pastor Dan? And worse, what if he believed her? Her blood ran cold at the thought, and she couldn't quite keep the tremor from her voice.

"Daddy, there's a problem at the parsonage."

Frank Edwards laid his pencil down and leaned back in his chair. His brows furrowing in concern as the story began, looked like two dark thunderclouds as the tale unfolded.

"You say, you saw Pastor Dan with his hands all over her." The muscle in her dad's jaw jumped just like it had when her brother Joe had wrecked the new car.

Tami shifted uncomfortably and nodded. Well, the pastor's hands had been around Faith's shoulders and arms. So, "all over her" would be technically correct.

"And you say Dan Whitman got in a fight with Hank Lundegard?"

"That's what Lisa said," Tami said, wondering why her dad was so focused on Pastor Dan. It was Faith Richards who was the problem. If her dad could have Dan throw Faith out of the parsonage, everything would be fine.

"Dad, about Faith Richards—"

"Honey, I don't have much control over what that woman does." Frank reached for the phone and sighed deeply. "But Pastor Whitman is another story. I must say I'm disappointed. I never would have expected such behavior from him."

"But Dad—"

"Tami, honey, why don't you go have some cookies with your mother? She spent all afternoon baking them. I have some phone calls to make."

Tami reluctantly stood. "Who are you calling?"

"The Board of Elders. We need to meet immediately and discuss which way to go with all this."

"You need to meet just to decide if Faith Richards should leave the parsonage?"

Her father shook his head, his fingers already starting to dial. "No. On what we should do about Daniel Whitman."

"Pastor Dan?" Her heart sank and for a moment she thought she might be sick.

His gaze softened. "I know how much you admired him, honey. But you did the right thing in coming to me."

The door closed shut behind her, and Tami leaned her head against the cool plasterboard wall.

Dear God, what had she done?

Dan limped into the parlor and heaved a big sigh as he settled down on the couch, propping his ankle up on the leather hassock.

Faith looked up from her needlepoint. "Did you hurt your ankle?"

"I got roped into playing a game of touch football with the boys next door."

She couldn't keep the smile from her lips. "And?"

Dan chuckled. "And Jimmy, the youngest, forgot what we were playing and tackled me."

She set her canvas on the table. "Maybe the doctor should take a look at it."

"Naw, it'll be fine."

She shot him a quirky grin. "How 'bout some peas?"

"I think Aunt Dora has already started dinner."

Faith shook her head. "Not to eat—"

"Oh, for the ankle."

"I'll get the bag."

When she walked past, his fingers wrapped around the dark fabric of her sleeve. "You don't have to, you know."

Impulsively Faith leaned down and brushed a kiss across his lips. "But I want to."

"Faith—"

She pulled from his grasp. "First things first. Let's get that ankle iced down, then—"

The ring of the phone interrupted her words.

"I'll get it, Aunt Dora," she called out. She reached for the receiver and giggled when Dan refused to let go of her arm. "Hello."

"Frank Edwards here." The curt voice took away her smile. "May I speak with Pastor Whitman?"

Faith frowned and covered the mouthpiece with her hand. "It's Frank Edwards."

She handed Dan the cordless phone and headed for the kitchen.

When she returned from the kitchen, the bag of peas in hand, the phone was sitting on the end table. Dan's eyes were closed and his head rested against the back of the chair.

She carefully wrapped the peas around his bare ankle, but when she tickled the bottom of his foot with her finger, he didn't react.

"Dan, is something wrong?"

"You might say that."

A flicker of apprehension coursed through her.

"What did Mr. Edwards want?"

Dan's gaze caught and held hers, his blue eyes now a flat and lifeless gray. "He called to inform me I've been accused of sexual misconduct."

A soft gasp escaped her. A suffocating sensation tightened her throat.

"With who?" she finally managed to choke out.

He let out a long audible breath and leaned forward, brushing his fingers softly against her cheek. "With you."

Chapter Sixteen

"Sexual misconduct?" A cold knot formed in Faith's stomach. "We never *did* anything."

"We kissed." Dan tossed the peas aside and raked his fingers through his hair.

"I don't think this is about kissing."

He stared up at the ceiling before lowering his gaze to meet hers. "I'm not going to worry about it."

"But this is ridiculous. You need to know the allegations. You need to prepare a defense."

He squeezed her hand and forced a smile. "I'm sure it's just a misunderstanding."

He obviously thought since he hadn't done anything wrong, everything would be okay. She'd believed that once.

"Did Mr. Edwards give you *any* specifics?"

"No, he just said that we were meeting tomorrow."

His tone made it clear he considered the subject closed. She pressed on. "Why don't you call him back and get some more information? That way you'll have time to—"

"Faith—" he said, a hint of warning running through his tone "—drop it."

She pulled away from his grasp and wrapped her arms about her. Despite the warmth of the house, an icy cold invaded her body. She sighed. "Dan, do you remember I told you I used to teach school?"

He nodded and seemed glad to change the subject. "I remember. You got laid off or something right around the time your parents died."

Faith ran her fingers along the table's edge, her gaze focused down. "If you recall, I never said I was laid off. I said I lost my job."

"Same difference," he said and then paused. "Faith?"

"Not quite the same," she said. "I was given a choice—resign or be fired."

"Fired?" Dan's eyebrow lifted. "Why?"

"Sexual misconduct," she said quickly before she lost her nerve.

"I don't believe it."

"Then you're in the minority. Denny made it so believable, even my friends thought it was true."

"Denny?"

"He was—is—the vice principal at the school I used to teach at. Married, active in the church, lovely wife and two adorable little boys."

"What happened?"

Faith took a deep breath. "Denny had always been friendly. After school he'd usually stop by my classroom and we'd talk. Since he was my supervisor I didn't think anything about it. Until—until he kissed me."

Dan's lips tightened into a thin line.

"I was so surprised, I just froze." She paused for a moment. "I told him he'd better not do it again. He just laughed. Said he knew I'd enjoyed it as much as he did."

Her gaze turned to Dan. "But I didn't want him to do it. He was a married man. You believe me, don't you?"

He shot her a reassuring smile. "Of course I do."

"After that I went out of my way to avoid him. Until one night I stayed late to grade papers and my car wouldn't start. Denny offered me a ride."

She closed her eyes, her heart pounding. Dear God, she didn't want to remember.

"Faith?" Dan's eyes filled with concern. "We can talk about this some other time."

She opened her eyes and took a deep breath. Her fingers pushed back her hair, now damp with sweat. Later might be too late.

"He stopped on a dark street. Then—" she swallowed hard against the lump in her throat "—he tried to force himself on me."

Dan's hands clenched into fists at his side. "If he hurt you—"

She gave a nervous little laugh. "No. I was lucky. Somehow I managed to get out of the car. When I wouldn't get back in, he drove off and left me there."

Dan's face was hard as granite. "I could see him being fired, but why you?"

"Remember the saying 'the best defense is a good offense?' Denny got to the principal first. Told him I'd been coming on to him even though I knew he was married. Said the final straw was when I acted like my car broke down in an attempt to get him alone. And—into my bed." Her heart clenched at the memory.

"My parents were flying back to help me fight the allegations. After their deaths…" Faith took a deep breath and blinked back the tears she refused to let fall. "All I'm saying is, I put too much faith in the system. And in my own innocence."

Dan's steady gaze met hers. "You were new to the school. I've lived here my whole life. God knows we did nothing wrong and I'm sure the elders will agree."

She hoped with all her heart he was right.

A hint of drizzle clung to the truck's windshield as Faith headed back to the parsonage. She'd spent the morning running errands: picking up mail at the post office, dropping off a birthday cake to a nursing home resident, even delivering a book to Harold that she could have just as easily dropped off with the sermon tape on Monday.

Busywork. Anything to keep her mind off the fact that this was the morning Dan met with the church council.

Her gaze listlessly surveyed the countryside. Leaves, which only weeks before had been vivid reds and yellows, now hung lifeless, dry and brown on barren trees. Those that had already fallen swept across the highway in gusts of autumn wind.

The cool chill in the air added the perfect touch to the gray-skyed day. Faith shivered. Her black leather jacket was not able to keep out the cold that rose from deep in her bones. She flipped the heater to high and turned the vents so the air blew her way. Along with the warmth came a faint hint of musk, the manly aroma permeating the confined space. Faith's heart clenched.

Dan. In the span of less than a month, he had insinuated himself in her life as tightly as the stitches in her needlepoint. Her eyes traveled the interior of the truck, now as familiar to her as her tiny import back home. There were reminders of the man everywhere—from the old church bulletin on the faded red dash to his well-worn leather gloves, always tossed in the same careless manner across the seat.

Her fingers reached over, bringing the soft cowhide to her cheek. The scent of leather and the man who wore them intermingled. Faith blinked back sudden tears.

Dear God, don't let anything bad happen to him.

She started at the brisk tap on her window. Her eyes widened. She'd driven to the parsonage, parked the truck and shut it off without even realizing what she was doing.

Dora stood outside. The thick woolen shawl clutched tightly around her thin shoulders was no match for the brisk air.

Faith cracked the window. "Dora, it's freezing out here."

"I thought something might be wrong. You've sat here for the longest time."

Dora's sharp eyes traveled over her and Faith knew, despite her declining vision, the matriarch missed nothing. Not the red, swollen eyes. Not the wobbly smile.

Faith heaved a resigned sigh and pushed open the door. Dan hadn't wanted to mention anything to Dora about the allegations, but Faith knew she'd have no choice but to tell her.

She put her arm around the older woman and they walked to the house. Faith steadied the frail body against her own.

Faith closed the front door firmly, blocking the harsh wind. When Dora insisted on hanging up her shawl on the cloak stand in the foyer, Faith frowned. The woman's lips were almost blue and goose bumps blanketed the spindly arms.

She propelled the older woman straight to her favorite wooden rocker near the fire. Despite Dora's protests that she was just fine, Faith took the quilt from the stand in the living room and tucked it firmly around the woman.

"You're already trembling, Aunt Dora. I don't want you to catch a cold because of me."

"You're a sweet girl, Faith," Dora said, pulling the quilt tightly around her. "I can't tell you how much I've enjoyed having you here."

Faith leaned against the mantel and swallowed hard against the lump in her throat. It wasn't just Dan she would miss.

She steadied herself, grateful when the teapot that Dora had set to heat on the stove whistled and gave her something to do besides think. By the time she returned from the kitchen with the serving tray, she finally trusted herself to answer.

"It's not me you'll miss," she said, forcing a teasing tone into her voice. "It's this mean cup of tea. Not everyone can boil water like I can."

Faith set the teapot and bags of tea on the rustic table next to Aunt Dora. The fifty-year-old alabaster china cups gleamed like new in the dim light. "You take a sip of this. It'll warm you right up."

Aunt Dora raised the cup to her lips, but didn't take a sip. "This isn't just a regular council meeting, is it?

Faith shook her head and reached for one of the scones Aunt Dora had baked that morning.

"No, it's not." The usually delicious pastry might as well have been sawdust against her tongue.

The pale blue depths stared at Faith unblinkingly. "Tell me what's going on."

Taking a deep breath, Faith raised her eyes to meet the wise gaze then stalled for time. "How do you know something's wrong?"

Aunt Dora settled her cup down with a clatter. "Because, my dear, I know you. Oh, I'm well aware we don't go way back, but with some people, when you meet them it's like you've known them forever."

Faith understood perfectly. Like Dan. Though she'd tried to deny it, from the very beginning there had been a special bond between the two of them. A bond that began as a slender thread but had grown thicker and tighter with each passing week. She closed her eyes momentarily against the pain.

Dora straightened in her chair, and even at eighty-plus years, the woman cut an imposing figure, the strength that had carried her through the death of her husband and other life tragedies visible in the determined face. "Tell me what's wrong."

Guilt washed over Faith. If only she hadn't kissed him. If only she hadn't fallen in love with him. If only...

"Faith?" Dora's eyes filled with compassion. "Tell me what's going on."

Trying hard to be clear and concise, Faith relayed the events of the past few days.

"Improprieties, eh?" The woman's eyes were sharp and assessing. "Any truth to the charges?"

Faith's face warmed. "We've kissed a—a few times. That's all."

"Nothing else?" A tiny smile lifted the corners of Dora's lips. "I've seen the way you two look at each other."

Faith shook her head. "Nothing else happened. I don't believe in premarital sex. And neither does Dan."

"Oh, so you've talked about marriage." A satisfied gleam shone in the woman's eyes.

"No, we haven't." She thought back. "Dan's made it very clear that he has no time for romance or marriage."

Dora shook her head in disgust. "What are we going to do with that man?"

"Nothing. At least I'm not." Faith took a deep breath then plunged ahead. "I'm leaving Willow Hill, Aunt Dora."

"But your motorbike…"

"It's fixed."

"Fixed? It can't be fixed. Ray—"

Her questioning gaze riveted to the woman. "It was your doing…."

"Indeed it was, and I won't apologize for it. You

two are perfect for each other.'' Dora took a sip of tea and studied Faith thoughtfully. ''I could see that from the beginning. You just needed some time.''

''Dora, matchmaking isn't—''

''Pshaw.'' A thin bony hand silenced her words. ''Now, you're sounding like my Herbert. He always said the same thing. Then I'd have to remind him of all the couples in town that were living happy married lives because I gave them a little push in the right direction.''

''I guess you have to strike out sometimes.''

''Oh, my dear, I never give up this easily.''

''Well, I'm afraid in this case you'll have to. I'm leaving Willow Hill. Today. And I won't be back.''

A shadow of alarm touched the wrinkled face. ''What about Daniel?''

''What about him?'' Faith shifted uneasily in her chair.

''You're leaving him, just when he needs you the most?'' Uncertainty shadowed Dora's features.

Faith forced a light smile to her lips, inwardly cringing at the disappointment reflected in the pale eyes.

''He'll be fine. I'm hoping with me gone things will return to normal.''

''So, you're going to run off and leave him,'' Dora said as if Faith had never spoken. Her thin fingers picked at the quilt on her lap and she sighed heavily, looking suddenly all of eighty-five. ''Just when he needs you most.''

"He has lots of friends."

"Yes, he does," Dora conceded. "But none that will understand what he's going through, like you will."

Faith's head jerked up. Dora almost sounded like she knew. But how could she? Even so, Faith thought back to those dark days when Denny had made those wild accusations and knew what the older woman said made sense. "Okay, I'll stay until this is resolved."

A satisfied gleam shone in the woman's eyes. "You, Daniel and the Lord. An unbeatable combination."

Faith sent a quick prayer heavenward. "I hope so, Dora. I really hope so."

Faith turned off onto the road that circled Willow Hill Lake, driving with extra care on the fresh gravel. The final meeting of the entire council wouldn't be over for hours, so she had plenty of time to hike off some tension on one of the lake's walking trails before Dan got home.

The truck rounded the corner and started to slide. Grateful she'd kept the speed to twenty-five, Faith quickly brought the pickup under control. An instant before she accelerated, a glint of cherry-red metal caught her eye. She hit the brake and wheeled the truck to the edge of the road.

Half-hidden by the tall weeds, a VW Beetle lay on its side in the ditch. Only one person in town drove this brand-new vehicle. Faith flung open the door. She eased down the steep incline and jerked open the crumpled door.

"Faith?" Blood trickled down Tami Edwards's cheek.

Faith forced a reassuring smile even while her stomach churned at the blood-splattered interior. "Are you hurt?"

"Just my head. I think."

Faith reached into her pocket and pulled out a clean tissue. She took a deep breath and pressed it firmly against an ugly gash on the girl's cheek. "You'll be just fine. I'm going to get some help."

"Lisa?" Tami's voice rose to a hysterical pitch. "She's not moving!"

For the first time, Faith realized Tami hadn't been alone. A still form was visible from beneath a twisted seat.

Faith took a deep breath and reached across Tami to grab the limp wrist. Her fingers searched and finally located a weak pulse. Relief flooded her.

"Is she dead?" Tami's scream blasted her ears.

Faith kept her voice low and controlled. "No, she's breathing on her own. She probably just has a concussion. Her pulse is good and strong."

The lie achieved the desired results. Tami relaxed.

"If I only had a cellular phone," Faith muttered under her breath.

"I've got one," Tami said. "It's in my purse."

Faith grabbed the bag from the back seat, reached inside it for the small phone and punched out 9-1-1. Her heart pounded so loudly, she wondered if she'd be able to hear the operator.

Emergency services answered immediately and Faith relayed the location and the condition of the two girls.

"Lisa's going to be all right, isn't she?" Tami's worried voice broke into her thoughts.

Faith slipped off her jacket and wrapped it around Tami. "You bet she will. While we're waiting, how 'bout we say a little prayer for her?"

Tami nodded and Faith started the prayer. "Dear Father in Heaven, please—"

"I'm—I'm sorry for what I did."

"Shh…" Faith brushed the girl's hair back from her face. "We don't have to talk about that now."

"Yes, we do." Tears filled Tami's eyes. "I was wrong to say those things. And now my own dad won't believe the truth."

Faith paused. Maybe it was best to let Tami talk. At least, it might help keep her calm. "What do you mean, he won't believe you?"

"I told him I'd made it up about you and Pastor Dan, but he said—" Two big tears slipped down the young girl's face "—he said that it was nice of me to try to stand up for Pastor Dan, 'cause he knew how much I admired him, but…"

Faith reached over and brushed away the tears,

sudden compassion filling her heart at the pain reflected on the teen's face. "But?"

"But that Dan would have to pay the price for his behavior." Her gaze shifted to Faith's. "You've got to believe me. I never wanted Pastor Dan to be hurt by any of this."

Faith thought for a moment. "Why did you do it, Tami? Why did you lie in the first place?"

Tami's lower lip trembled. "I don't know."

"Sure you do."

Tami turned beseeching eyes to Faith. "I—I love Pastor Dan. I just wanted you to leave. I never wanted to hurt him. Or you."

"But you did hurt him. You realize this could cost Dan a lot more than just his job," Faith said.

"I know. And I feel bad. I really do. But I can't tell my father why I lied. I just can't."

"You have the strength to do what's right."

"I can't. I want to, but I can't," Tami replied in a small frightened voice, fresh tears spilling against the bloodstained cheeks.

Faith closed her eyes and prayed. So much rested on this girl's decision. The choice Tami made now would affect her in the years to come.

"Tami, listen. God's always beside you, to give you strength to do what's right. You don't have to do this alone."

"I'm scared," Tami whispered.

Faith took the young girl's hands in her own.

"You know what? I've been running scared, too. But we both need to face our fears."

Tami finally nodded. "I'll try."

The ambulance and fire truck roared to a stop. The din of sirens cut off her words. Faith shot Tami a smile and moved aside.

Working quickly, the paramedics loaded the girls into the waiting ambulance and the vehicle took off, sirens blaring.

Faith watched the ambulance fade into the distance, and a sense of calm and resolution settled over her. With renewed strength, she climbed into the truck.

The hospital waiting room door stood ajar. Faith peered through the slight opening and caught a glimpse of a well-dressed couple deep in conversation with a man in a white lab coat. Even from a distance, the woman's uncanny resemblance to Tami convinced Faith she'd come to the right place.

It wasn't until after the ambulance had left, that Faith noticed she still had Tami's cell phone. She knew she could return it at any time, but she had a desperate need to find out how the girls were doing, and this was as good of an excuse as any. All the way to the hospital in Norfolk, she'd debated the pros and cons of showing up.

But now she was here and it would be stupid to continue to stand out in the hall. Faith squared her shoulders, pushed open the door and stepped inside. The three in the corner didn't even look up.

Faith glanced around the room and realized there was one person she'd failed to see. Off to the side, staring out the window and looking very much alone, stood Hank Lundegard.

Her heart went out to him, and without a second thought she crossed the room.

"Hank." She softly touched his sleeve.

"Faith." He turned and the look of welcome in his eyes made her trip worthwhile. "I sure am glad to see you."

"I had to come," she said simply. "How is Lisa?"

Hank jerked his head in the direction of the man in the lab coat. "That's the doctor over there talkin' to Frank and Joan. He told me Lisa's awake and he says he thinks she's goin' to be okay."

"I'm so glad." Faith breathed a prayer of thanks. "Lisa is such a sweet girl."

"She's my life." Hank's voice broke, and he swiped a hand across his eyes. "I don't know what I'd do without her."

"I'm sorry to interrupt." Frank Edwards tapped Hank on the back. "The doctor had to leave to make rounds. He said for us to wait here."

Hank blinked and drew a ragged breath. He didn't bother to turn around. Faith realized it was so that Frank couldn't see his tears. Giving Faith's arm a squeeze, Hank turned on his heel. He headed straight for the door, tossing the words over his shoulder as if he needed a nicotine fix in the worst way. "I'm goin' out for a quick smoke. I'll be back."

"Don't stay too long." Joan Edwards might have been only a few years older than Hank but she sounded more like his mother than a peer.

Faith hid a smile. Hank was lucky it wasn't cold out or Joan would be insisting he take a jacket.

With Hank gone, the man's gaze shifted to Faith. "Ms. Richards?"

Faith nodded.

"I don't believe we've met before. We're Tami's parents. I'm Frank Edwards and this is my wife, Joan."

She glanced at the outstretched hand. This man had brought the charges against Dan, an action that could cost Dan his job. She knew she should hate Frank but she couldn't. He was Tami's father, and regardless of how he'd treated Dan, the troubled eyes behind his steel-rimmed glasses told her how much he loved his daughter.

Faith took his hand. "Dan has mentioned your name so many times I feel I already know you."

A flush of red colored the man's cheeks and he hesitated, seemingly at a loss for words.

"Faith." Joan Edwards stepped forward and gave Faith an unexpected hug. "Thank you so much for taking such good care of our daughter."

"I didn't—"

"Tami told us how you found them. How you called for help and stayed until the paramedics arrived."

"It was nothing." Faith shifted, uncomfortable with the praise. All she'd done was punch 9-1-1 on a cell phone. Faith paused, then dug deep into her bag. She pulled out the tiny black square and handed it apologetically to Joan. "This is Tami's. The ambulance left before I realized I still had it."

"Don't worry about that. A phone, a car, they're nothing. Not compared to our daughter." Joan's lips trembled and Frank took her hand.

"The doctor said things might have turned out differently if you hadn't found the girls when you did," Frank said. "We don't know how to thank you."

"I'm glad I could help," Faith said. "It was just lucky that I decided to drive around the lake."

"I've been thinking about that," Hank said from the doorway. Like a shadow, the smell of tobacco followed him into the room. "I've decided that God had this all in the works months ago. He was the One that spooked that deer and made it cross the road in front of your bike. He sent you here so you could help my Lisa."

Faith started to tell him she couldn't imagine God having a hand in crashing her cycle, but the more she thought about it, the more she couldn't deny it.

Her stay in Willow Hill had restored her faith

and given her the opportunity to serve God in so many ways, including helping Lisa and Tami.

"You know, Hank, you may be right." Faith looked at him and smiled. "After all, the Lord does work in mysterious ways."

Chapter Seventeen

Faith opened the oven door, the rush of heat bringing a flush to her cheeks. The fork tines easily pricked the potatoes and Faith added just a little more salt and pepper to the roast before shutting the door.

It had been years since she'd prepared more than a simple one-course meal, and she'd pulled out all the stops tonight. Tonight's dinner would be her way of saying thank-you to Dan for his hospitality. And goodbye.

Now at peace with herself and her God, she'd be moving on as soon as the charges against him were dropped. He wasn't ready for a relationship and she wouldn't press the issue.

I can say that now, Faith thought. Ask me again when those blue eyes are gazing into mine.

The screen door slamming brought her back from her reverie and she took off the apron, her fingers reaching up to smooth a wayward curl.

"Something smells good in here." Dan leaned against the doorframe, his arms crossed. A smile creased his lips and he inhaled deeply.

Her heart lurched in her chest, and she longed to wrap her arms around him and beg him to hold her, knowing it wouldn't be much longer. Instead she smiled and kept her voice casual. "Running a little late this evening?"

He answered her smile with one of his own and sauntered past her, heading straight for the stove. He shot her a quick wink and she realized the stress and strain that had been etched into his features had vanished.

An impish grin stole over his handsome face, and before she could react, his finger dipped and swabbed a dollop of chocolate frosting off the top of her homemade cake. She batted at his hand, but like a recalcitrant six-year-old, he'd already moved on. Opening the oven door, a piece of the mouthwatering beef she had roasting made its way to his mouth.

Automatically her hand followed the meat to his lips. "Hey, wait a minute. That's for din—"

He turned and the words died in her throat. He grasped her hand and placed a kiss in her palm.

"Thank you," he said softly.

"For what?" she whispered. Her resolve to keep her distance melted in the kitchen's heat.

"For talking to Tami."

"Did she tell her dad the truth?"

"She sure did," he said, a smile teasing his lips. "And Hank cleared your name. Said there had never been anything between you and him. Told me later that you had eyes for only one man and that was me."

He touched her face with the back of his hand, caressing her cheek. "Is Hank right? Do you only have eyes for me?"

Faith swallowed hard at the teasing tone. She took a deep breath and stepped back. "What I have my eye on is the clock. Dinner will be on the table in a few minutes. Wash your hands."

The self-assured smile never wavered, although for a second Faith wondered if it dimmed. Until a moment later when he laughed and joked about Hank being wrapped around her little finger.

"I'm just glad his daughter is all right. And, of course Tami, too," she said, setting their places at the kitchen table.

His gaze followed her movements. He tilted his brow. "I'm banished from the dining room?"

"We're eating in here tonight."

"Good. I prefer the kitchen."

So did Faith. That's why she'd chosen to have the meal in the cozy intimate setting that held so many special memories. When she remembered

Dan Whitman in the years to come, it would be in this kitchen. Fighting over the carafe of coffee, tasting each other's eggs, sharing a bite of toast.

"Did I tell you my Harley is fixed?" She put the last of the silverware down.

Dan's head jerked up. "Done completely? Like ready to go?"

She nodded and tried to keep her voice light. "Yep, that's what Ray said."

She turned her back to him and prayed for strength. "I'll be leaving soon so I thought this could be sort of...well, sort of a farewell dinner."

"Why do you have to leave?" His voice reverberated in the silence.

"Well, there's really nothing keeping me here." She took a deep breath and wondered again why she'd chosen to put herself through this pain. "After all, your work is your life. You said so yourself. You don't have time for anything, or anyone else. That's what you said, wasn't it?

His expression stilled and grew serious. He took so long to answer, she wondered for a moment if he'd forgotten the question. "Yes. That's what I said."

"Is that still the way you feel?" She spoke quickly, before she lost her nerve.

He sighed deeply and laced his fingers together. When his gaze met hers, the answer shone in his eyes.

She shrugged, proud that her words came out

matter-of-factly as if they were discussing the weather and not their future together. "I just wanted to make sure I understood the way things were between—between us."

"Faith, I care for you very much."

A stabbing pain lanced her heart. She raised one hand. "No need to say more, Dan. We both have our lives to lead."

"Where will you go once you leave here?"

What do you care? she wanted to scream. But that wouldn't be fair. He'd never promised her anything but his friendship. It was she who wanted more. Ached for more. Not him.

"I'm going to head back to Kansas City and stand up for myself." She gave a little laugh. "Restore my good name. Then I'm not sure."

"Do you think you'll stay in Kansas City?"

Faith shook her head, "No, I don't think so. Since I've been here, I've come to realize I enjoy small-town living. Knowing your neighbors, working together. All that stuff. So I may look at teaching in a more rural school."

"You could teach here. The principal is always looking—"

"Dan, no." Her voice cracked. She took a deep breath. "It's better if I go somewhere else."

"Better for who? For you?"

Her eyes widened at his belligerent tone. "Dan…"

"We want you to stay. Aunt Dora loves you. The

kids love you. You could help with Youth Group, get involved in the church. Why won't you even consider it?''

Because, she'd like to yell at the top of her lungs, because it would tear my heart in two to be in the same town with you. Tears filled her eyes, but she determinedly brushed them aside. ''I just can't, Dan.''

''Well, that's not good enough. I don't want your dinner. I'm not going to sit here and act like everything is okay between us when it isn't. I'm going out.'' He grabbed his coat from the hook and stormed out. The door slammed shut behind him.

Faith stood in stunned silence. Tears that she'd kept hugged tightly inside, slipped down her cheeks one by one. She determinedly squared her shoulders and started picking up the tableware and returning the dishes to the cupboards.

Our last dinner together... She stifled a sob. Not only did he not love her, he didn't even like her. Faith covered her face and gave vent to the agony of her loss. She cried until she could cry no more, for a love that she knew now would never be.

The Harley gleamed in the fluorescent glare and the chrome glistened. And the miraculous changes weren't just cosmetic. Ray flicked the ignition and the cycle roared to life then settled into a soft purr.

''Ray, it's beautiful. Thank you so much.'' Faith flung her arms around the stunned mechanic's neck.

The smell of grease mixed with the floral scent of her perfume.

Ray awkwardly patted her back and started to pull away. "You're welcome, Missy. Glad to do it."

She felt a tap on her shoulder and turned. Hank Lundegard stood with his arms open and a grin on his face. "Got a goodbye hug for ol' Hank?"

Faith hesitated then shrugged. She held her breath against the smell of stale tobacco and alcohol that was as much a part of Hank as his lascivious grin and let his arms wrap around her.

Her eyes glanced over his shoulder, widening at the sight of the man in the doorway.

She stiffened and pushed Hank back. He reluctantly loosened his hold.

Ray raised his hand in greeting and waved the minister into the garage. "Pastor Dan. You're just in time. We're ready to launch the Harley."

Hank turned, one hand still resting atop her shoulder. "Mornin', Pastor. I was just getting ready to tell Faith here how we're all gonna miss her."

Dan's eyes hardened, though his smile never wavered. "Good morning, everyone."

Hank glanced back and forth between Faith's tense expression and Dan's inscrutable one. A knowing smile lit his features.

"How 'bout you, Preacher? You gonna miss your pretty little houseguest?"

Faith blushed.

Dan's firm jaw clenched and the line of his mouth tightened a fraction more, but when he looked back at Hank he said smoothly, "Of course we will. Both Aunt Dora and myself have enjoyed having Faith stay with us."

"I bet you'll miss her." One corner of Hank's mouth twisted upward. "Tell me, was it really true what I heard, that she was warmin' your bed over there at the parsonage?"

Faith took a step back, a soft gasp escaping her lips.

The punch came out of nowhere. Hank staggered, reeling from the hit.

Dan stood, his eyes flashing, his hands clenched into fists at his side. "Don't you ever talk about her in that manner. Faith Richards is a lady in every sense of the word. Do I make myself clear?"

An unexpected warmth surged through her. This unpredictable man had surprised her once again.

His hand still rubbing his jaw, Hank threw back his head and let out a great guffaw.

"I knew it." The room rang with his triumphant laughter. "All this civilized talk can't hide the fact that you love her as much as she loves you!"

Hank cocked his head questioningly. "The only thing I can't figure is why you're lettin' her go. Not that it's any of my business...."

"You're right about that," Dan said curtly. "It isn't any of your business."

Faith expelled the breath she'd been holding.

When Dan turned to her, his blue eyes pierced the distance between them. "I trust you'll be stopping by the house before you leave, to say a proper goodbye to Aunt Dora. I know she'll be disappointed if you don't."

"I'm not leaving until tomorrow morning."

His lips twisted in a semblance of a smile and he gave her a grudging nod. "Good."

"No hard feelings, eh, Pastor?" Hank grinned.

Dan stared at Hank, the lines of concentration deepening along his brows and under his eyes.

"No hard feelings," Dan said finally, his voice losing its steely edge.

"You pack a mean wallop for a man of the cloth," Hank said, his voice filled with awe and respect. "Where'd you learn to hit like that?"

Ray laughed, the raspy voice chiding, "Hank Lundegard, you got Alzheimer's or what? Dan Whitman was a Golden Gloves boxer during high school. That's not been that long ago."

The mechanic rubbed his whisker-stubbled jaw. "When I saw what you was doin', I thought, Hank, you better be careful, but you just went right on."

"I was just havin' a little fun, Ray. Just 'cause a fella's a preacher, doesn't mean he can't have a little honey."

"Hank." Dan's voice, though quiet, had an ominous quality.

"Oh, don't get your shorts in a wad. I'm only

sayin' that marriage may not be for me, but for you, well, you're crazy to let Faith go.''

"Well, thank you for your matrimonial advice, Hank." A hint of a smile touched Dan's lips and the tenseness in the room dissolved. "I'll keep it in mind."

"You do that." Hank rubbed his jaw and shook his head, a new respect in his voice. "Golden Gloves. Imagine that."

Faith fluffed her slightly damp hair with her fingers, the disheveled tendrils encircling her head like a black aura. Her image in the wavery mirror reflected her inner turmoil. A slight flush marred her ivory complexion and her jade-green eyes stared back at her, solemn and sad. Her black leather pants and jacket felt strange against her skin.

She pushed back a wayward strand of hair and glanced around the tiny bedroom one last time. The lace curtains, the gingham comforter that warmed her during the brisk fall nights, even the antique dresser seemed like old friends. She ran her fingers along the smooth walnut finish. Her room.

Not for much longer, she reminded herself. Faith straightened her shoulders and reached down to zip the olive-green duffel bag she'd packed this morning. A brightly wrapped package caught her eye and she pulled it out and placed it on the dresser along with a note to Aunt Dora. The thought of Sue

Perry's face when she got her ring back brought the first smile of the morning to her face.

Her gaze lingered on the Bible at the bedside. Last night, when she'd reflected back on the unexpected events that led to her detour in Willow Hill, she recognized God's hand. Meeting Dan Whitman had been a turning point in her life. Perhaps one day she would be able to think of him and be grateful, rather than filled with such pain.

The minute she started down the steps, she saw him. Dressed in her favorite blue wool sweater, the sight of him still had the power to take her breath away. Faith paused for a moment, using the time to regain her composure.

He gestured toward the parlor. "Do you have a few minutes?"

She nodded and moved past him into the room. Red flames crackled in the fireplace, but Faith shivered as she sat down.

Dan sat next to her. The familiar scent of musk wafted about him and Faith suppressed a groan. Her favorite sweater, that enticing cologne—if she didn't know any better, she'd think he'd decided to pull out all the stops. She fought the hope welling inside her.

Ask me to stay.

"I've done a lot of thinking. I haven't been very nice to you—" He raised his hand to silence her protest. "It's just the thought of you leaving tears me apart."

"We all make choices in life."

"I'll miss you."

"And I'll miss you." She drew a ragged breath. "Dan, I can't stay and just be your friend. I can't. I need more than that."

His silence gave her the answer she didn't want to hear.

Faith rose and this time he made no move to stop her. She put one foot in front of the other and somehow made it outside. She fired up the big Hog, eased out of the drive and didn't look back.

Chapter Eighteen

November 20

Dear Aunt Dora,

I enjoyed your recent letter. I'm glad to hear everyone is doing well, although I'm a little concerned to hear Dan is losing weight. He's sent me some letters, but I have to admit I've not opened them.

My trip to South Dakota was short but sweet. My uncle was thrilled with his Harley. Tell Ray Uncle George said he did a top-notch job on the repairs!

Kansas City is still the same, although I find I'm less tolerant of the traffic and noise. I stopped by the high school where

I used to teach, and was happy to learn that the vice principal had been discharged! I realize that may not sound very Christian, but if you knew this man, you would understand. All I'll say is he'd not been a gentleman to me, and apparently a similar incident with another teacher led to his termination. I'm only sorry I wasn't able to add my two cents to his dismissal. The principal is pressing me to accept a teaching contract but at this time I'm not sure what I'll do.

Our church circle is serving Thanksgiving dinner at a homeless shelter. The holidays can be a lonely time for us all.

I treasure your letters and I hope you'll write again soon.

Love always,
Faith

"What do you mean she's not opened my letters?"

"Just what I said. She wrote me back and said—" Dora reached for her reading glasses and picked up the one-page note she'd conveniently left out for Dan's visit "—here it is, 'He's sent me some letters but I have to admit I've not opened them.'"

She fluttered the letter enticingly in front of him, "Here. See for yourself if you don't believe me."

Dan reached for the paper, his mouth set in a tight grim line. He quickly scanned the letter.

"So, Denny finally got what he deserved," he mused, rubbing his chin thoughtfully.

"Denny?" Dora's pale blue eyes shone with youthful curiosity that belied her years.

"The vice principal," Dan said simply.

"Oh, so you knew all about him——" she lifted the letter from Dan's hand and peered down at the words again "——not being a gentleman."

"We talked about it some." He raked his fingers through his hair, still unable to believe she hadn't even opened his letters.

Tilting her head, Dora shot a slanted look at him. "It seems unusual, shall we say, that she'd confide in you something so personal and yet, now, not even read your letters."

Exactly his thought. Dan fought the odd twinge of disappointment laden with a heavy dose of irritation. He'd worked hard on those letters. Keeping them light and interesting. Avoiding any controversial topics. He never mentioned how lonely he'd been after she'd left.

His appetite vanished overnight. Eating alone just wasn't much fun. He'd find himself sitting at the breakfast table listening for her footsteps on the stairs.

Was she so selfish she didn't care that he was suffering?

"For fifty cents, I'd go down to Kansas City and give her a piece of my mind," he muttered, half to himself.

Dora's fingers rummaged through the pockets of her housedress, finally pulling two quarters from the depths. "Here, be my guest."

She tried to press the money into his hands. He chuckled and waved her money aside. He'd made his choice. What he'd told Faith still held true. He had no time for romance. And he certainly didn't have time to continue missing someone who didn't have the courtesy to open, let alone answer, his letters.

December 11

Dear Tami,

Congrats on making student council again this year!

Homecoming sounded like it was a lot of fun. I agree, Tommy Perkins is very cool, but I'm not sure I agree with you that he's better looking than Pastor Dan. Although you're right, Dan is getting old.

I'm glad Lisa was able to get rid of her crutches and dance at Homecoming. Tell her and Amy that I said hello.

Thanksgiving made me realize all I have to

be thankful for. I pulled a double shift at a homeless shelter with another lady from my church and it was one of the best Thanksgivings I'd ever had. Joe—he's eighty-five—said we were like God's angels on earth.

In answer to your question, no, I don't think I'll be back in Willow Hill for Christmas. Our church choir will be singing Christmas Eve and then I'll probably just go back to my apartment, put on some Christmas carols and eat a box of chocolates!

I still haven't decided whether to renew my apartment lease in February. Regardless, I won't be returning to Willow Hill. It's time to start a new life, forge new relationships. Right?

Write again soon and tell everyone hello from me.

Love,
Faith

"Pastor Dan." Tami waved at him across the snow-packed street. Her mittened hands cupped her rosy mouth like a microphone. "Come here a minute."

Dan hunched his shoulders against the icy chill and crossed against the light.

"Tami. Tommy." Dan acknowledged the tall, dark-haired youth with his hand resting lightly around Tami's shoulders. Faith had been right about that match.

Another Aunt Dora in the making.

He shrugged aside his sadness and gestured to the café, its windows frosted with steam. "You two have time for a quick cup of cocoa?"

Tami crooked her elbow through Dan's arm. "Hot chocolate sounds good to me."

"I'd like to, Pastor, but I've got some stuff to do. I gotta run," Tommy said, giving Tami's shoulder an apologetic squeeze. "Maybe another time?"

"Sure, Tommy." Dan smiled as the boy took off down the street. Like a lean and lanky colt, the teen loped at an almost rhythmic pace down the empty sidewalk.

Dan and Tami moved indoors and sat down. Across the chipped Formica table, Tami leaned forward, her elbows resting on the top. Dan could tell she had something on her mind by her intense expression. Sometimes he wondered how he'd failed to see her crush on him. She'd looked at him then with the same look she now reserved for Tommy Perkins.

"I got a letter from Faith," Tami said.

Dan kept his voice offhand. "That's nice. How's she doing?"

Tami took another sip of the steaming cocoa before she answered. "Great. Just great. She, uh, got together with a group of people for Thanksgiving.

Might even go over to their, uh, house at Christmas, too.''

He swallowed hard and wondered why he couldn't feel glad for her. "Really?"

"Guys were there, too. It wasn't just women."

A lump settled in Dan's stomach. "Anyone special?"

Tami tilted her head and one finger touched her mouth. "Let me see, did she mention anyone special? There was one guy. I think his name was Joe. She said they'd spent the holiday together, but she didn't say for sure they were dating."

"What do you mean, they spent the holiday together?" Dan said so loudly, the people in the next booth turned and stared. He lowered his voice several decibels. "Faith told Dora she was spending Thanksgiving serving dinner in a homeless shelter. What happened to those plans?"

Tami shrugged. "Don't ask me."

"So she spent the holiday with this guy. This Joe. What else did she say?"

Tami's blue eyes grew large and luminous. "I can't really remember. All I know for sure is they spent Thanksgiving together at his...at his house, and that—oh, now I remember—he called her his 'angel.' Isn't that sweet?" Tami rested her chin on her hand and stared up into his eyes.

Dan's brow furrowed. First Dora's letter and now this. "Real sweet. So, is she spending Christmas with this guy?"

Tami chewed on her lip and stirred the whipped cream into her cocoa, before shaking her head. "Umm, I'm not positive. You know she wrote a lot. It's really hard for me to remember everything she said."

Dan glanced out the window, then down at his watch. He thrust a couple of bills onto the table. "Well, I'd better get going. I'll see you Sunday."

Tami smiled sweetly. "Pastor Dan, I'll make sure I let you know the next time I get a letter from Faith. You do the same, okay?"

He stopped and inhaled a deep breath. "Sure."

Dan walked toward his house, almost relishing the biting cold. The stiff wind numbed his skin, forcing his body to shift its focus from the pain deep inside.

He forged ahead, the promise of a hot shower and a blazing furnace like a dangling carrot in front of him. Once he warmed up, he'd settle in next to the roaring fire with a steaming cup of coffee. Alone.

The word nipped at the façade that he'd so carefully erected when he'd let the woman he loved walk out of his life. For two months he'd been telling himself that with her gone, his life could get back to normal. If he'd been honest, he'd have had to admit that normal meant having her in his life. Two people who loved each other and led separate lives wasn't normal.

Why had he been so insistent he didn't have time for a wife? Since Faith had left, there'd been countless times he'd longed for her wit, her smile, her caring. And many situations in which she would have been such an asset in the ministry. After all, couldn't two Christians do more working together, than one alone?

Dear Lord, why did I ever let her go?

Aunt Dora called him stubborn. The day Faith left, she accused him of not using the sense God gave him. He'd tried hard to make her see how a relationship with Faith didn't fit into his plans.

Her pale eyes had flashed. "I don't want to know about *your* plans, Daniel Whitman. I want to know what God's plans are for you and Faith."

He'd tried to tell her about his plans for the church. Furthering God's kingdom. It would take time....

She'd interrupted him, her lips set in a thin fine line, her fingers resting on her hips. "God's plan, Daniel. Not your plans."

When he'd tried to explain again, she'd thrown up her hands in disgust. "You just don't get it, do you?"

Dan now pushed open the door to the empty house, only a blast of warm air to greet him. He shrugged off the down-filled parka, scattering ice crystals across the floor.

Instead of heading upstairs to the shower, he made his way to the kitchen, not even bothering to turn on the lights. The fading light outside was enough to illuminate the dim halls.

A note from Aunt Dora stood propped on the table. He scanned the flowery cursive print before he tossed the paper back on the counter. Her church circle was having their annual Christmas party. Cold cuts and leftovers were waiting in the fridge for him.

He sat down at the table.

God's plans.

The words echoed over and over like a stuck record in his head until he finally understood what Dora meant. He'd set goals and made decisions based on *his* plans. What God thought of a union between him and Faith Richards, he honestly didn't know. He'd never asked. A deep sense of shame swept over him.

Dan folded his hands and bowed his head, the questions tumbling forth from his troubled heart. A sense of peace stole over him. He raised his face to the light.

Aunt Dora had been right all along. Love came in God's time, not according to Daniel Whitman's personal agenda. He knew now what he had to do.

The clock on the shelf chimed ten o'clock. Faith carefully hung up the ivory-colored crepe dress she'd worn to the New Year's Eve church service.

She plopped down on the bed, clad only in her undergarments and nylons and massaged her aching feet. The heels had been stylish but uncomfortable, like most fashionable footwear. It had taken all her willpower not to ease them from her feet during the service. With one deft gesture she flung them into her open closet, breathing a sigh of relief as they fell into the dark corner. It would be a long time before she'd go looking for that pair.

The clock on the television counted down the end of the year. Faith plopped back on the bed, the memories of the last twelve months bringing a wry smile to her face.

How quickly everything could change. The minister's message on that very topic could have been directed straight to her. As the sermon unfolded, his words hit a responsive chord. Earthly comforts, such as people, possessions, friendships can be gone in the blink of an eye. The Lord was the one constant.

She shivered, remembering all too well how she'd almost cast her faith aside. Her stay in Willow Hill had God's mark all over it. The accident, staying with Dan and Aunt Dora, the incident with Tami—it all had served its purpose. It would be a stronger Faith, with God at her side, who would face this world.

But all I want is Willow Hill.

On the dresser, an envelope with pink pigs around the border caught her eye. Underneath was a gray envelope imprinted with Dora's name. Letters from home.

She loved hearing the local gossip. The only hard part involved Dan Whitman. Tami and Aunt Dora sprinkled his name throughout their letters. She could see him now, standing at the pulpit, his blue eyes filled with passion as he brought God's word to his congregation.

She missed him more with each passing day. Time hadn't made it any easier. Neither had the tapes.

Faith had found them the first time she unpacked her bag after leaving Willow Hill. Five sermon tapes shoved deep in the bottom of her bag, courtesy of Aunt Dora.

Three weeks she resisted. Until Thanksgiving. The apartment seemed particularly empty and the loneliness overwhelming. On a whim she'd plopped one of the cassettes into her stereo.

She couldn't believe how good—and how hard— it was to hear that rich baritone again. Her heart turned over every time he used the word *faith*. She'd listened to all five services that night and fell asleep to the sound of his voice, sleeping soundly for the first time in weeks.

Listening quickly became a nighttime ritual. Pull on the sweats, heat up the hot cocoa and relax to the sound of Dan's voice.

Faith glanced at the clock again. She still had time to play one before the Times Square countdown.

Comfortably attired in sweatpants, T-shirt and

slippers, Faith padded to the kitchen. Automatically her hands reached under the stove for the small saucepan. Without even needing to measure, she poured in some milk and set the heat to medium. The tapes were out, the afghan ready for her to snuggle under. All stood in readiness. One last time.

This would be it. She'd made the difficult decision weeks ago. Her New Year's resolution was to move forward with her life. Listening to Dan Whitman every night made that impossible. She poured the near-boiling liquid into the tall blue cup, mixed in the cocoa and splurged with a handful of marshmallows.

Tonight she'd listen to her favorite of the five tapes: a wedding sermon with Dan talking on love and lifelong Christian commitment. It could be disastrous. She hoped it would be cleansing.

She cranked up the stereo volume and his voice filled the room, the words going straight to her heart. A shiver rippled down her spine.

Dear Lord, I still love him. She expelled a heavy sigh and closed her eyes.

The knock at the door came as no surprise. She grabbed the remote and guiltily lowered the volume to a more neighborly level. After tonight, the other tenants would never have to complain again.

She jerked open the door. "Look, I'm sorry about the noise."

Her fingers moved to her mouth and she took a step back. "Dan, what are you doing here?"

"I know it's late." His smile never wavered, although he shifted uneasily from side to side. "Can I come in for a minute?"

"Yes, of course." Faith moved to the side, opening the door a little wider to let him pass.

"Did I catch you at a bad time? What in the—?" A puzzled look stole over his features.

The tape! Like red lightning, a flush bolted up Faith's neck. She hit the remote.

A smile quirked at the edges of Dan's lips. "That guy... He sounded like a mighty good preacher."

"Aunt Dora gave me the tapes," Faith said stiffly.

"I'm glad," Dan said. "I wondered if you'd forgotten all about me."

She bit her lip and shook her head. "That's not easy to do."

"You didn't write." He studied her face with his enigmatic gaze for an extra beat.

"I didn't even read your letters," she admitted.

"Why not?"

She lowered her lashes. "It would have been too hard," she said softly, almost to herself.

"Oh, Faith." Dan held out his hand.

Her heart raced, and tempted though she was, she crossed her arms across her chest and took a step back. It wasn't fair. She'd just made up her mind to try to get over him.

His hand dropped. "I've something I want to tell you. Mind if I sit down?"

She uncrossed her arms long enough to gesture toward the sofa. A flicker of apprehension coursed through her. "Aunt Dora? Is she—"

"She's fine," he quickly reassured her. He unzipped his rust-colored parka and sat down, leisurely stretching his long legs out in front of him.

Faith studied him as he glanced around her small apartment. His jeans molded against his legs and the Nordic blue sweater hugged his broad shoulders. Stubborn blond tendrils lay against his forehead. Those blue eyes still had the power. Her heart fluttered in her chest.

"You've got a nice place here."

"I'm moving next month," she said. Her fingers played with the doily at the top of the chair. "I've already given my notice."

"Where are you going?"

Faith shook her head and gave a little laugh. "I don't really know. I just didn't want to be here anymore."

As strange as it sounded, it was the truth. She'd prayed for guidance, and last week she'd told Principal Jeffers she wouldn't be accepting a second-semester contract. That same day, she'd given her thirty-day notice on her apartment. The time had come to move on.

Dan's gaze grew thoughtful but he didn't comment. His eyes settled on her rapidly cooling cup of hot chocolate and she could almost see him switch gears. He quirked his brow questioningly, a boyish smile on his lips. "Got one of those for me?"

"Coming right up." She bustled into the kitchen, glad to have something to do. Her hands trembled as she poured the milk. She heard the television click on.

"We don't have long before the ball drops."

It was like old times. She took a deep breath, her fingers gripping the counter edge. Why was he here?

She handed him the cup of cocoa—made with two marshmallows, just the way he liked—and sank into the recliner, drawing one leg up underneath her.

"Why are you here, Dan?" she said bluntly.

He set the cup down slowly, his eyes rising to meet hers. "To see you."

Faith's temper soared. "Why are you doing this? Don't you realize how hard this is for me?"

He rose and she waited for him to zip his coat and walk out the door. Instead he knelt down beside her. His warm hands enfolded her cold ones. "I love you, Faith. I've made a lot of mistakes. The biggest one was when I let you walk out of my life. I want to spend the rest of my life with you. I want you to marry me."

Tears slipped down her cheeks but she didn't take her hands from his. "But what about your plans?"

"My plans..." Dan half chuckled. "For a while

I'd forgotten that the only plans that matter are God's plans.''

He raised one finger to her face, softly tracing the wetness. ''The Lord brought us together, Faith. I know that now. And if you'll marry me, I'll spend every day making you happy.''

A warmth spread outward to her fingers and toes. Her heart thumped erratically and more tears slid from her eyes.

A worried frown stole over his handsome features. His fingers reached up and cupped her chin, tilting her head back. ''Faith, sweetheart, what's the matter? Don't you want to marry me?''

''Oh, Dan, of course I do. I love you so much.'' She flung her arms around his neck, pulling him close. ''Just promise me I'm not dreaming.''

''If it's a dream, then let's both never wake up.'' He held her tight against his chest.

''Hey, look.'' Faith swiveled in his embrace. The roar of the crowd in Times Square filled the tiny living room. The frenzied throng were counting down the final seconds to midnight. The huge metal ball was ready to begin its descent.

''Happy New Year, Faith,'' Dan whispered, his breath hot against her cheek. ''And to many more....''

His lips when they captured hers were wet with tears. Whose they were, hers or his, Faith couldn't tell. All she knew was God had brought them together, and for that and so much more, she would spend the rest of her life giving Him thanks and praise.

Epilogue

Two years later

Faith Whitman quickly swirled the last of the chocolate frosting onto the birthday cake. In less than an hour friends and family would arrive to celebrate little Dora's first birthday.

The door to the kitchen opened and Faith glanced up. Aunt Dora stood smiling with the toddler in her arms. The little girl's golden hair stuck up from her head in fine puffs, her porcelain-blue eyes lighting with pleasure at the sight of her mother.

Aunt Dora set her down on the floor next to Faith and handed her some toys hidden in the voluminous pockets of her housedress.

Little Dora squealed with delight, her chubby fingers curling around a tiny doll made of yarn.

Aunt Dora smiled down at her namesake, her expression turning serious. "How was your doctor's appointment?"

Faith dropped her gaze to the cake. For the past months, it had become a great chore to get out of bed in the morning. And, even with sleeping late, she'd found herself falling asleep over the evening news. She'd almost convinced herself it was no more than any busy mother would experience, when the nausea arrived. This morning she'd finally given in and seen Doc Stewart.

When he'd sat down beside her after the exam and taken her hand, Faith thought she might faint.

She hesitated. She didn't want to hurt the woman's feelings, but she wanted Dan to be the first to know the diagnosis.

The outside screen door slammed and her husband's voice rang through the house. "Faith, I'm home."

"We're in the kitchen," Dora hollered.

Dan strolled into the room and shot her a questioning glance. Last night, when she mentioned she might cancel her doctor's appointment, he'd pulled her into his lap, his fingers closing over hers, his blue eyes dark and serious. "Promise me you'll keep it. I want you to find out what's going on."

She'd nodded, but he'd noticed her trembling lips and pulled her head down against his chest, cradling her in his arms as he often did their daughter. "What's worrying you?"

"What if it's something bad? I've been gaining weight, even though I'm hardly eating. What if it's something serious—" she whispered, her voice breaking.

His body tightened and he took a deep breath. "I'm sure it's not, but if it would be, then we'll deal with it. Together."

His hand stroked the back of her head. "I'll always be here for you, sweetheart. Better for worse, sickness or health, those weren't just words for me."

They hadn't been just words for her, either. When they'd said their vows in front of his congregation almost two years ago, her words had come straight from the heart. Tears stung the back of her eyes. "I love you, Dan."

"Faith?" She glanced up to find Dan and Aunt Dora staring worriedly at her.

"We asked, what did the doctor say?" Aunt Dora repeated, tapping her cane against the floor.

Dan's brow creased, his eyes solemn. "Did Doc Stewart find anything?"

Remembering the doctor's words, Faith raised a trembling hand to brush back a stray tendril of hair.

"Faith, we're your family. You can tell us." Normally strong and confident, Aunt Dora's voice shook.

Dan pulled a chair up beside her and sat down, lifting their daughter up on his lap. He bounced the baby up and down on his knee, her gurgles of pleasure lightening the atmosphere. The little girl was a carbon copy of her handsome father. Faith's breath caught in her throat and tears filled her eyes.

"Faith, whatever it is—" he added, in a lower, huskier tone.

She reached out then and covered his hand with hers. "Doc ran some blood tests and did an exam. When he told me the diagnosis, I said that was impossible, but he said—"

"Faith—" Dan interrupted her. "What did the doctor say?"

"I'm pregnant," she said quickly. "Four months already."

"But how—" Dan's voice broke off midsentence.

"Wonderful news." Aunt Dora nodded her head in approval and shot Dan a look of reproach. "Little Dora needs a playmate."

Faith took a deep breath. "That's not all. We're having twins."

A soft gasp escaped Dan's lips. "Two?"

Aunt Dora clapped her hands. "Two babies. Even better. A double blessing."

"Baby." Little Dora patted her chubby hands together imitating her namesake. "Baby."

Dan glanced from little Dora to Faith, his gaze returning to rest on his daughter. His blue eyes softened and he smiled. "Yes, Dora. We're going to have two babies."

"You don't mind?" Faith whispered, her hand

on her chest. She knew this meant many of his plans for the upcoming year would have to be put on hold.

"If you remember, I already learned that lesson." He chuckled and the tenderness in his expression warmed her heart. "God's plans beat my own every day. The Lord's blessed me with a wonderful wife and daughter, and now we'll be blessed again. I'm surprised, but I couldn't be more pleased."

He leaned forward and kissed her softly on the cheek, the gesture bringing tears to her eyes.

The tap of Aunt Dora's cane once again resounded throughout the kitchen. "You've got plenty of time for that later. Right now we've got a birthday to celebrate."

Faith's eyes shifted from Dan and the baby to Aunt Dora. She smiled, taking in the faces of her family, so familiar and so dear.

Dan had been so right. God's plans came first, and as long as they kept Him in the forefront of their lives, they would always be truly blessed.

Her hand moved unconsciously to her rounded abdomen and she breathed a prayer of thanks for all her blessings.

* * * * *

Dear Reader,

Have you ever mapped out a plan for your life only to find out God has a different plan for you? Have you ever been touched by tragedy and, in hurt and anger, abandoned your faith?

In *Unforgettable Faith,* Pastor Dan Whitman is a man who has some personal goals for his ministry and nothing is going to get in his way. Romance? He doesn't have the time. Dan, however, comes to realize that things happen in "God's time," not his own.

When the sudden senseless deaths of her parents are followed by the undeserved loss of her beloved teaching job, Faith Richards has had enough. She is through with God. But God's not through with her. And He's never through with us!

I hope you enjoy reading this book and watching these characters learn and grow in their faith while they struggle with very real day-to-day issues.

With warm good wishes,

Cynthia Rutledge